# Would you Rather?

# Chris Higgins

*h*

Hodder
Children's
Books

A division of Hachette Children's Books

A Catalogue record for this book is available
from the British Library

ISBN 978 0 340 97076 8

Typeset in Bembo by Avon DataSet Ltd,
Bidford on Avon, Warwickshire

Printed and bound in Great Britain by Clays Ltd, St Ives plc

The paper and board used in this paperback by Hodder Children's
Books are natural recyclable products made from wood grown in
sustainable forests. The manufacturing processes conform to the
environmental regulations of the country of origin.

Hachette Children's Books
a division of Hachette Children's Books
338 Euston Road, London NW1 3BH
An Hachette UK company
www.hachette.co.uk

Praise for *Would You Rather?* and Chris Higgins

'The characters are very individual. This is a great book and I would recommend it.' Ella, 11

'The book was extremely gripping and truly unique. The storyline was really good and made the book impossible to put down . . . No one could possibly not like this book.' Elly, 13

'I thought the book was written very well. The story was really gripping and the twist of events made me want to read on and on. I read this book in a day – it was really good I couldn't put it down!!' Beth, 13

'I loved the way it started. It sounded like me!' Sophie, 12

'Chris Higgins writes in a dead-on emulation of a teenage girl's voice, her prose salted with pithy observations.' *Financial Times*

'Higgins packs a lot into an easily-read book, taking the issues seriously but presenting them with a welcome lightness of touch.' *Books for Keeps*

'. . . convincingly captures the teenager's view of the world.' Julia Eccleshare, *Lovereading4kids*

'She has a light touch and an easy style that absorbs you right from the very start.' *The Bookbag*

*Other books by Chris Higgins*

32C That's Me
Pride and Penalties
It's a 50/50 Thing
A Perfect Ten
Love ya Babe

For Zac

Thanks to Twig, Kate, Pippa, Claire and Lucy.

And to Lindsey, Anne and Naomi.

And Georgia for the title.

Amy and I have been messing about in my room all afternoon. We've gone through our favourite playlist, prancing along in front of the full-length mirror, me singing into my hairbrush, Amy wailing into the hair straighteners. We've run through our old dance routines and tried out some new ones and now we've moved on to practising our flirting technique.

Actually, Amy is practising *her* flirting technique. She's keen on a boy at school who's a bit slow on the uptake. Me, I'm not too sure if I want to flirt at all. I don't think I'm ready to be *in lurve*, not since I've seen what it's done to Ezzie. Like Mum says, it's a messy business, romance, because it involves men.

Even flirting is complicated. Amy is explaining to me how she thinks Mitch likes her but he won't make the first move.

'You do it then.'

'What? Like me put my arm round him?'

'Yeah.'

'No way!'

'OK, be a bit more subtle. Say something to make him put his arm round you.'

'Right. Good idea.' She thinks for a minute then her face lights up. 'OK, I'm ready, let's give it a go.'

'What?'

'You be Mitch and I'll be me.'

'I'm not putting my arm around you!'

'I'm not asking you to! Well, I am, but as Mitch, not you. Come on, Flick, it's known as acting! Improvisation! You're good at that.'

'All right.' Amy always knows how to get around me. Flattery works every time. She beams at me, then strikes a pose, body hunched, shivering, arms wrapped around herself. Oh dear. She's such a ham actor.

'I'm freezing . . .' she whimpers.

'Put a jumper on then.'

'You're not supposed to say that!' she barks, falling immediately out of role.

'Why not? That's what Mitch would say!'

'No he wouldn't!' She thinks about it for a second and then says, honestly, 'Well, even if he would, you're not supposed to! You're supposed to be helping!'

'I am helping! Stay in role.'

She groans and collapses on to my bed, throwing her arm over her face, the picture of despair. 'There's no point,' she wails. 'It's not going to work. He doesn't even know I exist.'

'I thought you said he was just too shy to make the first move?'

'Oh, I don't know. Men!' She sighs deeply then rolls over and props herself up on her elbows. Her face breaks into a grin.

'Daddy or chips?'

'Chips!' This is the signal to play our favourite game. It came from a TV advert for oven chips. There was this really cute little kid with an older sister and an annoying dad. The dad kept pinching the cute kid's chips so the older sister says to her, 'Daddy or chips?' meaning, which one do you like best, and the cute kid thinks about it and answers truthfully, 'Chips.' Ezzie and I used to love this advert, because the dad in it was just like our dad and he used to pinch our chips too.

So we started up this game that is all about choices. They can be serious choices or silly ones, but the rule is, you have to think about them carefully, even if they're so ridiculous they make you roll about on the floor, shrieking with laughter.

But Ezzie hasn't felt like shrieking with laughter for a while so I've started playing it with Amy instead.

I have to admit, she's pretty good at it. Better than at acting, anyway.

'I've got a good one!' Amy sits upright. 'Ready?'

'Ready.'

*'Would you rather . . . have one huge eye in the middle of your forehead or three small eyes?'*

'Nice one!' I consider it carefully. 'Can I have two eyes at the front and one at the back?'

'No, they're all at the front.'

'Pity. Not so useful.' I think about it for a while, weighing up all the implications. 'I'd still be able to see more though. And I could rest one if it was tired.'

'You'd need a massive pair of sunglasses though.'

'A massive trio of glasses, you mean. That would be cool!'

'Hmm.' Amy's not convinced. 'Don't know if Specsavers do them. And anyway, what would you do if one of your eyes needed glasses and the others didn't?'

'Easy, I'd wear a contact lens. Or a monocle.'

Amy giggles. 'A monocle! That's funny. But think about it, you'd take forever getting ready to go out. You'd have three eyes to make up . . . eyeshadow, highlighter, liner, mascara . . . that's expensive too.' She thinks for a moment then says, 'No, I'm going for one. It's easier and cheaper.'

'I'm going for three. Then if anything happened to the other two I'd still have one left. And it would be useful for driving.'

'You can't drive.'

'I know, but I will one day. Ezzie's learning.'

'Is she? Is your dad teaching her?'

'No, he thinks she should have proper lessons to get her started. He and Mum booked her ten lessons for her seventeenth birthday. She's having one right now.'

'Lucky thing. I can't wait to learn to drive.'

Amy can't wait for anything. She lives life in the fast lane and she's always miles in front of me. Music, hair, fashion, gossip, she's up there in the know because she spends her life reading all the mags, watching TV and checking out the net. It's like she's programmed to Fast Forward and I'm programmed to Play.

Oh no, I sound really boring! I'm not, honest! I love doing stuff. I'm really good at acting and improvisation – everyone says so – and I love writing stories. One day I'm going to be a journalist or work in television, like Aunty Libby. But Amy will be the celeb and I'll be the one interviewing her.

I read my stories to Grandma Liz. She's my biggest fan. I've got two grannies, Grandma Liz and Grandma Fizz. Ezzie was named Elizabeth after Grandma Liz who's Dad's mother and I was named Felicity after Grandma

Fizz who's Mum's mother. We don't see much of Grandma Fizz because she lives in Scotland but Grandma Liz and Grandpa Bert live nearby so we see a lot of them.

We don't see anything of Aunty Libby though. She's my dad's older sister. She went off to university when my dad was little and never came back. I don't think I've ever met her and Dad can hardly remember her himself. She's really big in television now, though she's not a face you'd recognize. You see her name on the credits, she's a director. It must be so interesting, though personally I'd rather be in front of the camera. She worked her way up, Grandma says, and now she's really important.

It's a shame we don't see her. 'She's too busy,' Grandpa says and looks a bit sad. I don't think I'd ever be too busy to see my own mum and dad. Or my annoying little brother and his wife and their two amazing daughters. But then I'm not famous.

Yet.

We do get some seriously expensive birthday and Christmas presents though from Aunty Libby and Uncle Jay (he's American) and their kids, Sam and Ellie. Mum always feels she has to match them. I heard her moaning about it last Christmas as she wrapped up presents.

'Forking out for kids I've never even met,' she complained.

'Don't do it then,' said Dad, matter-of-fact as ever.

'Don't be stupid,' she muttered, tearing off Sellotape with her teeth. 'She's your sister!'

'She doesn't mean anything to me,' he said, shrugging his shoulders. 'I wouldn't know her if I bumped into her in Tesco's.'

'That's not the point,' said Mum crossly. 'Anyway, I bet she wouldn't be seen dead in Tesco's. She's more of a Selfridges person.'

'Is she?' I asked with interest.

'I don't know,' she shrugged. 'I've never met her.'

I'd love to meet her, my famous Aunty Libby.

I'd love to be on the telly too.

Fat chance.

'Your turn.' Amy prompts me back to the present. 'Daddy or chips?'

'OK.' I wander over to the window for inspiration and look down into the street. A car pulls up outside, with a Driving School sign on the roof. I watch as Ezzie gets out awkwardly and stands upright, rubbing her back.

*'Would you rather . . . have a baby in your teens or a baby in your forties?'*

'I'd rather not have one at all,' says Amy. 'I hate babies.'

'You've got to choose,' I say. 'It's the game.'

'I know that. When I'm in my forties. Definitely.

7

There's no way I'd want one now. I can't think of anything worse.'

Me neither.

'Yeah, forties,' I say emphatically. 'No contest. Come on, let's go downstairs. Ezzie's back.'

In the kitchen Mum and Grandma Liz are sitting at the table, drinking tea and flicking through a pile of holiday brochures showing pictures of wide stretches of white sand dotted with stripy parasols and impossibly blue seas. Mum's always doing this, it's a hobby of hers.

'Don't know why you bother,' I say, sitting down beside them. 'We never go anywhere.'

Mum looks up. 'I can live in hope. It's not for lack of trying. It's your dad's fault.'

'He never wants to go on holiday,' I explain to Amy. 'He says he does, but then he always makes excuses. Like he's got too much on at work. Or, when Buster was alive, he wouldn't put him into kennels.'

'Well,' Mum consoles, 'at least he hasn't got that excuse any more.'

After a moment's silence for Buster, our recently departed and deeply missed mongrel, I resume the attack. 'No, but now he says we can't afford it. Didn't stop him getting himself a season ticket for the footie though.'

'Martin's a home bird,' says Grandma fondly. 'Always has been.'

'It's not fair. I'm the only person in my class who's never been abroad,' I grumble. OK, I don't actually know if this is true or not. But most people do seem to go on foreign holidays and I've never even been to London!

'Never mind, Flick. When we leave school we can do a gap year together before uni. Go round the world,' says Amy.

'Yeah! We can backpack round Australia!'

'Go to America and swim with the dolphins!'

'Go to Peru and follow the Inca trail!'

'Can I come with you?' asks Mum.

'Whatever next!' laughs Grandma.

'We can be beach bums in Thailand!' I shriek, getting carried away.

'Or in the Caribbean! I've always wanted to go to the Caribbean.'

'We can visit Cambodia!'

'Where's Cambodia?'

'Next to Vietnam,' a voice says quietly. Ezzie has slipped in beside me like a wraith in a fog. Too late I realize it was her dreams I'd been shouting out. Silence falls across the table.

'Any tea left?' she asks and stretches forward to pick up the pot, her T-shirt riding up to display her back, still tanned from last summer's sun, and the elegant, tightly knotted line of her spine.

From behind you can't see the round, swelling mound of her stomach.

'I'll make some fresh,' says Grandma and takes the teapot gently from Ezzie's hand with a small, painful smile.

It's Ezzie's fault that I'm known as Flick. She couldn't manage Felicity when I was born. Well, it is a bit of a mouthful, isn't it? Felicity Pottery! Actually, I think she did me a favour, I'm more of a Flick than a Felicity, which means happiness, joy or rapture. That's a lot to live up to.

My sister is gorgeous. She reminds me of a graceful, startled gazelle, because she's slightly built, with impossibly long and slender legs and clear creamy skin, and she has wide brown eyes with sweeping, dark lashes. Gazelles are delicate and beautiful and spend their time in large herds.

Me, I'm more of a meerkat. They're those funny little creatures with long necks and little upturned noses that sit up on their haunches to see what's going on. They like living in large extended family groups and they're very inquisitive, constantly turning their heads from side to side so they don't miss a thing. That's me, that's what I do!

Though hair-wise, I'm different. I'm more like the grey crowned crane we saw in Edinburgh Zoo last year when we were on holiday. At least, that's what Dad said. He had a point. It had a crown of stiff golden feathers, not grey at all, which stood up round its head, just like mine. Lucky old me, I got to inherit Dad's frizz. His is dark and he keeps it cropped short, but mine is blonde and hovers around my head in a mad cloud. From the back I look like a dandelion clock.

Ezzie, I forgot to say, has straight fair hair that she got from Mum which she wears trailing sleekly down her back. Normally you would expect the ugly sister to hate the beautiful Cinderella but I don't. No one could hate Ezzie, she's lovely. She's so nice and kind, people gravitate around her, like bees to a honeypot. She sees the best in everyone and she's one of those people who picks up waifs and strays and I'm not just talking cats and dogs here, even though she was the one who brought Buster home all those years ago when he was a starved, shivering, cowering mutt and coaxed him back to exuberant life.

Maybe that's why she took up with Spud in the first place.

Poor Spud. She met him at college. He wasn't a

student, he was working in the kitchens. Trust Ezzie to start talking to him even though most people didn't even notice him in his white overalls with his dreadlocks hidden under a hairnet, swishing his damp cloth over the tables, clearing up everyone's mess.

She was going places, our Ezzie. She's a bit like Amy, on the go all the time, full of ideas, can't wait to get on with the next part of her life. But, unlike Amy, she's a planner. She had it all mapped out. A levels, university, career in some branch of medicine. Saving lives or saving souls, that's our Ezzie. But before that, as soon as her A levels were over, she would be off on her promised gap year with her mates as a reward for all her hard work. Thailand, Australia, New Zealand, Vietnam, Cambodia and finally South America, to work with street kids because she'd watched a documentary on the telly and wanted to go and help.

At first Spud was just another one in a long line of blokes Ezzie brought through the door. He was different from the usual fit, loudly confident students Ezzie normally brought home though. Different enough to make Dad's eyes widen with shock. 'Who the hell's that?' he asked as Spud, after a strangled 'All right?' disappeared upstairs behind Ezzie, long and stringy in his scruffy jeans and studded leather jacket, a row of rings through his left eyebrow, hair tied back into thick, matted coils.

'Spud,' I said. 'He's a mate of Ezzie's. From college.'

'Spud?' he said, shaking his head. 'What sort of name is that?' He turned to Mum and added, 'Not exactly a King Edward, is he?' For some reason they both considered this to be highly amusing.

'No,' I said. 'He works in the kitchens.'

Dad's eyebrows nearly shot through the top of his skull but Mum shook her head warningly: 'Cool it, Marty. It's just a phase.'

I don't know how long phases are supposed to last but I've got a feeling Mum thought it would be a matter of weeks and Dad hoped it would be a matter of minutes. Neither of them were right. Gradually Spud seemed to become a permanent fixture around the place, loping along behind Ezzie like a devoted greyhound. He was no trouble, as Mum pointed out. He never said much, though when he was in Ezzie's room with her you could hear them chatting and laughing together. We were all a bit surprised; he didn't seem Ezzie's type.

'He's not stopping her from getting on with her studies, is he?' asked Grandma who was round one night when Spud was leaving. Ezzie had gone outside with him to say goodnight. That's a euphemism for having a snog on the doorstep. I know because I've watched them out of my bedroom window.

'Don't think so,' said Mum. 'She stays in more

nowadays than she ever did. I don't think he can afford to take her out. He's not got much of a job.'

Grandma sniffed. 'She could do better than him,' she said.

'Liz!' warned Grandpa. 'It's nothing to do with you.'

'I'm just saying, that's all!'

'She's not going to marry him!' laughed Mum. 'You know Ezzie, she's got her future mapped out. It's different nowadays, they don't settle down like we did.'

'No, you know what girls are like,' said Dad, playing up to Grandpa. 'It's like shopping, see, Bert. See something, take it home, try it on, change your mind, take it back the next day. Our Ezzie'll get fed up with old Maris Piper soon and take him back to Tesco's. Swap him for a better class of spud.'

Grandpa chuckled. Dad took a big swig of beer and smacked his lips, looking pleased with himself as if he'd said something profound. Mum rolled her eyes at me then leaned over to pat Grandma on the arm.

'Don't you worry, Liz,' she said. 'It's not serious. She's off on her travels before long. It'll soon run its course.'

Grandma didn't look convinced. I remember when Ezzie came back in a couple of minutes later. Her face was flushed and she looked as if she was glowing inside. I'd never seen her look so happy.

She doesn't look happy now.

'How did the driving lesson go?' asks Mum.

'All right.' Ezzie studies her nails intently while a pulse beats visibly in her throat. She's trying not to cry, I can tell. A tear spills over and rolls treacherously down her cheek. She scrubs it away angrily.

'What's up?' asks Mum gently.

'Nothing!' she says, then, wildly, 'Everything!' Her face is wet now as the tears fall, fast and furious. Mum gets up and puts her arms round her and Ezzie turns into her, weeping.

'It's not fair!' she wails.

'No, it's not,' agrees Mum, patting her back. Grandma sits down with a fresh pot of tea. She looks as if she's going to cry too.

Poor Ezzie. Her life's on hold.

She'll do her A levels, all being well, but everything else has come to a halt. Gap year, travelling, university, medical career. Girly nights in, crazy nights out, skimpy tops, micro skirts. Gigs, pop festivals, beach parties, clubbing. Illicit cocktails, spicy curries, her favourite prawns, even an innocent cup of coffee. All gone.

She's going to have a baby. By Spud. Lanky, uncoordinated, inarticulate Spud with his scruffy studded leather jacket, strangled words and dreadlocks.

She didn't plan that one.

'What happened then?' asks Mum quietly, smoothing back Ezzie's hair from her tear-stained face.

She shrugs. 'Nothing really. John said I'd be better off putting in for my test after the baby's born. I know it makes sense. There's a big waiting list and it's already getting a tight squeeze behind the wheel. It's just one more thing . . .' Her voice trails away miserably.

'I know,' murmurs Mum. We all do. It's like Ezzie's life has come to a full stop, for the time being at least. The driving lessons were something for her to look forward to. She hardly goes out of the house any more, just to college, that's all. She still sees Spud occasionally, but not very often. That's another thing that's on hold. He's not really welcome at the house, Dad's livid with him.

'It takes two you know!' said Ezzie, defending him, like she would. And in case you're wondering why she didn't get rid of it, well, you'd have to know my sister to understand that she could never do that. It just wasn't an option.

So now she's saddled with an unwanted pregnancy.

It's put me off ever getting involved with anyone, I can tell you. I'm going to remain celibate, for ever.

I glance at Amy. She looks really upset seeing Ez in tears. Maybe she'll have second thoughts now about getting off with Mitch. Just as well, I wouldn't trust him.

Though it's not as if Spud has left Ezzie in the lurch, had his wicked way and abandoned her, like some evil villain in an old black and white film. It's not like that at all.

It's more like nobody knows quite what to do next.

Our English teacher gives us the title 'Trapped' and tells us to write a story for homework. I write one about a girl who is trapped in her life and wants out. She wants it so much she wishes for it every day. Strange things start happening to her. First she develops a zit on her forehead which slowly evolves into a horn. Then the skin on her hands and feet grows hard and calloused and her neck seems to be elongating. Her teeth and nostrils grow larger and she feels the urge to gallop everywhere. Slowly she realizes she's changing into a unicorn.

The trouble is no one believes her.

Eventually, she gallops so fast she takes off up into the sky. Soon she is flying over the rainbow and up, up, high above the stars. She has shaken off the confinements of her life and set herself free.

My teacher loves it. I get an A★. She makes me read it out to the class and they cheer and yell, 'Go, Flick!' and bang the desks at the end. I shine with pleasure. I'm not a meerkat any more, I'm a unicorn, a beautiful, magical creature.

I go round to Grandma's on my way home to read it to her. She's peeling vegetables for stew but she puts down the knife immediately, wipes her hands clean and sits down. She listens rapt as I read it out and at the end she gasps.

'Flick, that's marvellous,' she says. She turns to Grandpa who's just walked into the kitchen. 'Our Flick has written a new story,' she says.

Grandpa sits down and unfolds his newspaper. 'Well done.'

Grandma clicks her tongue crossly. 'Show a bit of interest then!'

'I am interested,' Grandpa says mildly. 'Flick knows that, don't you, love?'

''Course I do.'

'Read it again for Grandpa,' urges Grandma.

Grandpa puts the paper down patiently. I shake my head. 'No, it's all right.'

He winks at me and picks the paper up again. Poor Gramps. All he wants is a quiet life.

'See! You've put her off now!' Grandma's got the bit between her teeth today. 'She's got a gift, you know.'

Grandpa puts the paper down again. 'I know that.'

'Well then. Give her some encouragement.'

Stop going on, Gran. I'm beginning to wish I hadn't bothered.

'Everyone needs a bit of encouragement. Especially when you're as talented as our Flick. You're going to be a famous writer, aren't you, love?'

'I don't know about that . . .'

'Yes you are, you'll be as famous as your Aunty Libby one day, you mark my words.'

Grandma's on a mission. Aunty Libby's not that famous. Like no one my age has heard of her. *We* only see her name on the credits because we look for it.

'You're doing it again.' Grandpa's voice is quiet, but there's an edge to it, a warning. Grandma carries on regardless.

'She was clever, but she needed a push. Just like you. You've been given a talent, Flick. You must use it.'

'I know that, Gran.' My voice is defensive. What's it to do with her, anyway?

'Pushing!' says Grandpa crossly. 'You'll push her away, keeping on like that.' Grandma ignores him.

'Look at Ezzie,' she continues, her voice breaking. 'What a waste! What a terrible waste.'

'Be quiet, woman,' warns Grandpa.

'She should have that baby adopted!'

I stare at her, shocked.

'You know I'm right! She should have it adopted and get on with her life!'

'It's not your decision!' Grandpa folds up his paper and gets to his feet.

'Martin and Jo should tell her straight. It would be better off and so would she!'

'Now that's enough!' says Grandpa, raising his voice. 'You've said enough for one day.'

'She should go to university, become a doctor!'

'It's nothing to do with you, woman!' explodes Grandpa. 'For once and for all, will you stop interfering in other people's lives!'

I stand stock-still, horrified. I've never, in the whole of my life, heard my grandfather shout at my grandmother. Not once. They hardly ever have a cross word between them. Little niggles, yes. But nothing like this.

And Grandma. She's not serious, is she? She doesn't really want Ezzie to give her baby away, does she? Grandma who loves us all so much, who's so proud of us all. I can't believe she wants that.

Because, I suddenly realize, I don't.

I look at her, sitting at the kitchen table, her knuckles pressed tight against her mouth as if she's afraid of what's going to come out next. Part of me wants to go to her and give her a cuddle and say, 'It's all right, Gran, don't fret.'

But instead, I turn and run away from that house for the first time in my life.

When I get home, no one's in. The house is empty and cold and I feel alone and scared like I've taken a wrong turning and ended up somewhere strange. I fish around in the cupboard under the stairs till I find the Poorly Blanket, the one Mum used to swaddle us in when we were off school sick, and I wrap myself up inside it. I don't like it when there's no one at home.

It occurs to me that if Ezzie had been going off on her gap year as planned, this was something I would have had to get used to. Before long I would have been alone most days after school till Mum and Dad came home from work. At least I was going to have my sister around for a bit longer.

Then I remember what Grandma had said and my blood runs cold. Maybe Ezzie will have the baby adopted and go off anyway. I hadn't thought of that.

As if I've conjured her up, the front door opens and Ezzie walks in. She looks knackered.

'Why are you all wrapped up in a blanket?'

'I'm freezing,' I say, glad to see her. 'The heating's not timed to come on yet.'

'Advance it then,' she says, practical as ever. 'You're home early,' she adds, glancing at the clock.

'Grandma says you should have your baby adopted!' I blurt out.

Ezzie frowns. 'Does she now? Well, it's not her baby.'

'That's what Grandpa says. Are you going to, Ez?'

She shrugs. 'Nothing's decided yet.'

I stare at her in consternation. Ezzie sighs and collapses on to the sofa beside me. 'Budge up, nuisance,' she says and I shift up obediently. She picks up my hand and examines my nails intently.

'Is that my nail varnish?'

'Sorry.'

Ezzie bites her lip. 'Do you want me to?'

'No!' Silence. 'Do you?'

Ezzie ignores the question and continues to examine my hand as if it's sprouted talons.

'It's not just up to me, Flick.'

'What do you mean?'

'Well, it affects us all. Mum, Dad, you . . .'

'It's your baby,' I say, in a small voice. 'It's your choice.'

'Huh! Some choice!' she mutters bitterly then lapses into silence. After a while she says, moodily, 'It'll keep you awake all night, you know. Babies do.'

'I don't care.'

'You won't be able to have your friends round very often.'

'So? I only want Amy here anyway.'

'She won't come. The house will stink of sick and poo.'

No, you're right, I think morosely. Amy would hate it. Then, in spite of myself, I giggle.

*'Would you rather . . . the smell of sick or the smell of poo?'*

'Sick, every time!'

'Me too!'

Her face breaks into a smile. She's so pretty.

'Don't give it away, Ez,' I insist, quietly. 'You won't, will you?'

She exhales deeply, a long, sad sigh.

'Feel that.' She guides my hand to the ball of her stomach.

Beneath the palm of my hand I feel a sharp, insistent jolt, like when someone elbows you in the ribs. Just as I think I imagined it, it happens again. Ezzie laughs.

'You should see your face!'

'What are you two up to?' Mum comes in, shrugging off her work jacket and slinging it over the peg by the door. The jacket slips to the floor.

'Ezzie's baby kicked me!' I say in wonder.

'Did it?' she laughs. 'Let's have a feel!'

She squats down beside Ezzie and presses her hand on to her tummy, her face a picture of concentration.

'It's gone quiet,' says Ezzie, disappointed, then, 'There it is!'

'Oh yeah,' says Mum, smiling. 'Strong little blighter! There it goes again! You've got a little footballer in there, Ez.'

'Maybe,' says Ezzie, pulling the blanket off me. 'Might be a girl though.'

'It could still be a footballer!' I protest, tugging the blanket back and wrapping it round me. 'You're so sexist, Ezzie.'

'*You're so sexist, Ezzie!*' she mocks and tugs the blanket so hard it unwinds and I nearly topple off the sofa. I grab at her wildly to save myself, both of us shrieking with laughter.

'Careful, you two!' warns Mum. 'That's my grandchild in there!'

A rosy glow envelops me. Ezzie takes advantage and tips me on to the floor, then swathes herself triumphantly in the blanket, giggling her head off and managing to look smug at the same time.

'Why are you two fighting over a stupid blanket anyway?' says Mum, shaking her head. 'It's roasting in here.'

She's right, it is. Suddenly, home is a nice, warm place again.

Ezzie doesn't want to give her baby away, does she?

And even if she does, Mum's not going to let her, that's for sure.

'That's my grandchild in there!' she'd said.

It was Amy that showed me the competition in the first place. She was sorting out her bedroom one Saturday afternoon and I was giving her a hand because her mum had thrown a strop and said she couldn't go out till she'd fumigated it. Amy's mum is like mine, she does tend to overreact to a little light disarray. Amy had collected together a huge pile of mags and, you know what it's like, there's nothing so fascinating as old magazines. Even if you've read them, you've forgotten what was in them. So we'd tipped everything on to the floor and were taking an enforced break on the bed while we caught up with out-of-date celebrity gossip and last year's fashion tips.

I'm engrossed in an article about weird pets (weird owners, more like! I mean, who would really want to take a wolf for a walk?) when Amy goes, 'Hey, Flick, this is right up your street.'

I glance across at what she's reading. The word COMPETITION!!!!!!!!! meets my eyes in big bold capitals and a row of exclamation marks.

'I don't do competitions,' I say and go back to the weird pets, having just discovered that this crazy girl lets the wolf sleep at the foot of her bed. Amy sits bolt upright.

'No, listen. It's about writing. You're brilliant at writing. You have to write an account of a sports event you've been to.'

Actually, this does sound marginally more interesting than the lupine loony. 'How long does it have to be?' I struggle up to read the article with her, my arm round her shoulders.

'Umm . . . 800 words.'

'That's not much. What do you win?'

'Wow!' Amy's eyes round in excitement. 'If you're one of the four best entries, you get to go to the Television Centre in London and do an audition.'

'What for?'

'Hang on, I haven't got to that bit yet.' She scans the page. 'Oh my goodness, I don't believe this! It gets better and better! Listen to this. "The winner will go to a sports final of their choice to report on it for children's television. This could be anywhere within the European Union over the next six months!" '

'What's that mean, "within the European Union"?'

'Abroad, idiot! You get to go abroad! Wow! Do you think they'll let your best mate go with you for company?' She beams with excitement. '*And* you get to go on the telly.'

'Yeah, *if* I win!'

'You'll win, easy-peasy!'

Amy's enthusiasm is infectious. 'So, all I have to do is write 800 words? Are you sure?'

'Yeah, look, it says here.' We read it together. She's right. Amy looks up, her face shining. 'Go on, Flick, have a go. No one can write like you.'

It's what I want to do. Be a journalist or a television presenter. Or both. Suddenly, a thought occurs to me and I feel a stab of disappointment, like a knife in my guts.

'It's too late. These are old magazines. It'll be over by now.'

Amy turns back to the front page and peers at the date. 'It's two months old,' she says, looking worried.

'When's the closing date?'

She scrabbles back through the magazine till she finds the right page and scans down it. 'What date is it today?' she asks anxiously.

'Umm . . .' I grab a calendar off her desk. 'The fifteenth.'

'That's OK then, it's the seventeenth,' she says triumphantly.

'But it's Saturday!' I wail. 'It won't get there by Monday. The last post has gone.'

She points at the page. 'No, look! You can enter by email, it says here. There's still time!'

Suddenly this competition has become the most important thing in the world to us both. Amy jumps up and sweeps a pile of clutter off her desk to get to her computer. 'Do it now!' she commands.

I sit down obediently and turn on the computer. 'Password?'

'Mitch.'

Of course. I tap it in and configure to Word. A blank page appears before me.

'Right then,' I say. 'Here goes.'

Amy sits beside me. Everything is still. The minutes tick by. She gives a little cough of encouragement.

'What am I going to write about?' I ask.

'A sports event you've been to. Duh!'

'I haven't been to one.'

'Oh.'

We sit there, racking our brains.

'We could go and watch one this afternoon,' she suggests.

'Like what?'

'I dunno. The footie?'

'You need a ticket for that. Anyway, they're playing away. My dad went off on the supporters' coach this morning.'

'I know! I'll get the paper!' Amy leaps up and disappears. A couple of minutes later, she's back with the 'What's On?' guide from the local weekly newspaper.

'Now then . . .' She lays the paper on the bed and we scour through it together.

'There's yoga on in the Guildhall . . .' I suggest.

'What? A load of middle-aged women in tracky pants and trainers, lying about on rubber mats. I don't think so!'

'OK. What about the Ramblers then? What do they do?'

'They are so boring! It's just a bunch of pensioners out for a walk together. My nana goes sometimes.'

'There's a bowling match on the Green . . .'

'Puh-lease.'

'Well, I don't know! There's got to be something exciting going on round here . . .'

'Like what? Dog walkers white-water rafting down the canal? Shoppers bungee jumping off the roof of the multistorey car park? Traffic wardens playing beach volleyball in the High Street?'

Amy can be very negative sometimes.

'Nah, there's nothing going on, Flick.' She drops the paper to the floor. 'Never mind. It was a good idea while it lasted.'

I don't want to give up now. I really want to do this.

Suddenly, I have a brainwave!

'School's got matches on today, Ames! Zoe and Maya are playing in that knockout tournament, remember? It's going on all day. We can go and watch them.'

'Hockey?' Amy wails. 'I hate hockey! I don't want to spend Saturday afternoon watching a stupid hockey match.'

'It's not just hockey,' I remind her. 'It's footie too. The boys have got their own tournament on.'

Amy doesn't look convinced.

'Mitch is playing in it,' I add casually, hoping it's true.

Amy's face brightens up like someone's switched 2000 watts on inside her head. 'Come on then!' she says, flinging her wardrobe doors wide open. 'What shall I wear?'

Ten minutes later, we clatter down the stairs, Amy dressed in the most glamorous footie-watching outfit she could find, me clutching a notebook and pen.

'Hold on! Where do you think you're going?' yells Amy's mum from the kitchen.

'School, actually,' says Amy, cool as can be.

'On a Saturday?' Her mum comes out into the hall,

looking mega-suspicious.

'We've got special homework to do.' Amy indicates my notebook and pen. 'We've got to go to watch a football match and write about it.'

*We?* Since when did this become *we*?

Her mum shakes her head. 'I told you! You've got to tidy that room before you go out.'

'I've done it!' says Amy, adopting an injured look. 'Go and check if you don't believe me!'

We wait with bated breath as her mum climbs up the stairs. Two minutes later she's back down again.

'Can I go?' Amy asks sweetly.

Her mum nods. 'Not bad,' she concedes. 'Not bad at all.'

We're out that door in a split second and running up the street before she decides to investigate further.

We've made a wonderful, time-saving, low-energy, eco-friendly discovery.

It doesn't take long to tidy a room if you just bung everything into the wardrobe.

I go straight home after the footie final to type up my article. It was really good, by the way – we won. I read it over, save it, then get cold feet. It could do with a second opinion before I send it off. I want to try it out on Dad to see if I've done it right, but he's still out. Actually, thinking about it, that's not such a good idea after all. He'd probably go all technical on me and make me do a match report and that's not really what I want. I've gone more for atmosphere, excitement, the thrill of it all.

Because, let's face it, I don't know an awful lot about football. I can't even understand the offside rule. I stare at the words on the screen morosely. I bet it's rubbish.

I need to read it to Grandma.

I haven't spoken to her properly for ages. Not since the day she said Ezzie should have her baby adopted.

She shouldn't have said that.

But I don't hold grudges.

I pick up the phone.

'Grandma?'

'Flick!' She sounds so pleased to hear me, I feel ashamed for thinking badly of her.

'Can I read something to you?'

'Of course you can.'

Good old Grandma. She's always there when you need her.

It sounds better out loud. When I finish, I ask, tentatively, 'What do you think?'

There's a pause while Grandma considers.

'Well, I'm no expert on football; in fact, I don't even like it very much,' she says finally. 'But that article makes it sound exciting. It makes *me* want to go to a match and I never thought I'd ever say that.'

'Does it? Honestly?'

'Yes, honestly. Is it from the paper?'

'No,' I say proudly. 'I wrote it myself.'

'Oh my goodness! You are a clever girl!'

'Thanks, Grandma. It's for a competition.'

'Well you'll win, I'm sure of that.'

Ahh, Grandma. I would if you were judging it.

I text Amy for the details before I change my mind. She'd decided to hang around after the match, hoping to catch Mitch's attention. She needn't have bothered as it turned out.

She rings me back immediately.

'He didn't even notice me!' she wails. 'He just disappeared. D'you think he's gay?'

'Definitely not!' Neither would she if she'd seen what I'd seen on the way home. Just put the words 'Mitch', 'Zoe' and 'round the back of the changing rooms' together in the same sentence and you'll know what I mean. Best not to mention that to Amy though.

'He's just footie mad,' I say consolingly. 'That's all he's interested in. You know what blokes are like. Have you got that email address, Ames?'

'Zoe fancies him too, I know she does. I don't reckon he rates her though, do you?'

'Course not.' It's OK to tell a little white lie if it stops you hurting someone's feelings, isn't it? 'What did you say that address was?'

'Only I'd rather you tell me straight if you think she's in with a chance.'

I sigh. I'm never going to get this flipping address out of her until she's stopped obsessing about Mitch. 'OK then. I think I might have noticed them eyeing each other up once or twice . . .'

There's a stunned silence. Then a squeaky, wounded, little voice says, 'I can't believe you said that, Flick! You're supposed to be my best friend!'

Wrong move. 'You didn't let me finish!' I splutter. 'I

didn't say he fancied her! She just makes it obvious she likes him, that's all. Not like you! You're more . . .'

'More what?' she says suspiciously.

'Subtle!' I say, plucking a word from my brain. 'Subtle, that's what you are.'

Again there's silence. It crosses my mind she's not exactly sure what I mean by this. Neither am I. But I can't let her throw a strop on me; I need this address fast.

'She's so in his face,' I blither on. 'Not a bit like you.' OK, I'm into massive black lies now but this is an emergency. There's no time to waste.

'Do you think he fancies me then?'

'Definitely. Amy, about that email address . . . ?'

'So, I've just got to let him know I fancy him too, yeah?'

'Yes!'

'How?'

'I don't know!' Short of tattooing 'I'M AVAILABLE!' in big letters on her forehead, I think she's tried everything.

Amy sighs deeply. 'That's my problem, I'm too . . . subtle.' She tries the word out, sounding pleased with her new label.

'Absolutely. Amy, the competition. I need the—'

'OK, I've made up my mind. I'm going to drop the shyness, be a bit more assertive . . .'

Heaven help us! I take a deep breath and try some assertiveness myself.

'Amy!' I yell down the phone. 'If you don't give me that email address, I'm going to kill you!'

'OK! OK! You only had to ask!' she says in surprise. 'I'll have to dig through the wardrobe for the magazine. I'll text you back when I find it.'

She did, finally, on Sunday afternoon. It wasn't an easy task apparently, buried as it was under the piles of stuff we'd tossed into the wardrobe. Her mum came in while she was going through it all and went ballistic and she had to tidy everything away properly before she'd let her text me. She even nicked her phone off her until she'd done a proper job. Her mum's a bit harsh like that.

Maybe you need to be harsh if you're Amy's mum.

As soon as I get Amy's text, I send off my article. I knew I had zilch chance of winning, but the harder it became to meet the deadline, the more determined I became to get my entry in. It had become a real mission.

That done at last, I wander downstairs to see what's going on. Grandma and Grandpa have come around and everyone's reading the Sunday papers.

'Where's Ezzie?'

'Gone to meet Spud,' says Mum, her head buried in the travel section.

'Is that still going on?' asks Grandma, surprised.

'Who knows?' she says from behind the paper.

Grandma frowns. 'He should take responsibility.'

'Liz . . .' warns Grandpa, quietly.

Grandma sniffs. 'Well, he should.'

Mum lowers her paper. 'I think he wants to. It's our Ezzie who doesn't know what she wants.'

'Typical woman,' says Dad, jokingly, trying to lighten the atmosphere. Mum bites immediately.

'I know what *I* want, all right,' she says sharply. 'I want you to take me on a nice holiday, now you're off work for a fortnight, somewhere warm and sunny. I'm sick of this weather.'

'Where do you want to go then?' asks Dad, magnanimously. 'Go on, you name it. Brighton? Bournemouth? Clacton? You choose.'

'You can go right through the alphabet but you won't escape the rain this year,' says Grandpa gloomily.

'We will if we go to Lanzarote. Or Malaga. Or Cyprus.'

'Hark at her!' appeals Dad. 'She thinks I'm made of money!'

'It's no more expensive!' says Mum. 'I keep telling you. Look, here's one in Spain. It's cheap as chips! It costs less than a coach trip to flaming Scarborough. Read it yourself!' She thrusts the paper at Dad. Daddy or chips? flashes through my mind.

*Would you rather go on holiday to Spain or Scarborough?*
*Scarborough or Spain?*

No contest.

'Don't be daft!' mocks Dad, reading the advert. 'They just put those cheapies in to make you contact them, then they say they've gone and con you into buying a more expensive one.'

'No they don't!' Mum wrinkles up her face in derision. 'They're not allowed to do that. I've a good mind to ring up about it.'

'Go on, Mum! Give them a ring!'

'You won't get a holiday in Spain for that price, I'm telling you!' says Dad and rolls his eyes at Grandpa.

Big mistake.

'So if this holiday is available you'll go on it?' Mum's jaw has tightened.

He snorts. 'Yeah, if it's available at that price, we'll all go!'

'Go on, Mum!'

'Right then.' She reaches for the phone and punches the number in. Dad picks up the sports section again, looking smug, and Mum glares at him and settles down to wait, her mouth set in a determined straight line. After a while, someone must have answered because she sits up straight and starts rattling off details into the phone like she's used to jetting round the world every day of her life.

'How many people? Four.' She looks up at my grandparents. 'Six?' Grandma and Grandpa look at each other, then Grandpa nods. He's enjoying this.

'You can! Wonderful!' Mum hugs the phone to her chest with both hands, her face triumphant. 'They can do it for that price! We're off to Spain at the end of the week!'

'Yes!' I jump up and down, clapping like an idiot, beside myself with excitement.

Mum looks as if she's about to collapse with joy.

Dad looks as if he's about to collapse with heart failure.

'Give me the credit card, Martin!' instructs Mum. Dad opens his mouth to protest.

'Now!' says Mum grimly, her arm outstretched. Dad closes his mouth, digs into his back pocket and hands over his wallet without a word.

'Insurance? Yes, we'll want insurance.' Mum fishes the card out of the wallet, one-handed. 'Meals on the plane? Yes please . . . How much? Good grief! Hang on a minute, let me check.'

She raises her eyebrows at us all. 'Ten pounds each?'

Dad shakes his head furiously.

Grandma and I nod vigorously.

Grandpa chuckles away to himself.

'Oh, go on then, why not?' speaks Mum into the

phone. 'Meals for six, please. Yes, both ways.'

Dad whimpers softly.

'It's easy this,' whispers Mum, beaming at us all. 'She's ever so helpful. Her name's Sandra.' She carries on answering lots of questions to the ever-so-helpful Sandra on the end of the line, most of them concerning luggage and airport parking and transfers to the hotel and rooms with sea or pool views and all of them entailing extra charges to Dad's credit card bill. He, by this time, is slumping unbecomingly in his chair and fanning himself with the sports pages of the paper. Even Grandpa has stopped tittering to himself and is looking a bit alarmed. Mum doesn't notice though; she's on a roll, chattering away, nineteen to the dozen, to her new best mate.

Then all of a sudden she says, 'Passports? Um, yes, I think so. Hang on a minute.' She covers the mouthpiece with her hand. 'Liz? Bert? You've got passports, haven't you?'

They look at each other and nod.

'I haven't!' says Dad.

Mum swears. Then she looks at me and says, 'Damn! Flick hasn't got one either.' She speaks again into the phone. 'Actually, Sandra, not all of us have got one.'

Sandra jabbers away to her for what seems like a disproportionate length of time. Mum's smile fades.

'Pardon?' Her tone has changed. 'But we're not going till the end of the week!'

We can hear more jabbering. Mum looks as if she might have changed her opinion about the helpfulness of her telephone chum. Her eyebrows knit together in a frown and I discover I'm holding my breath.

'How long will that take then?' she asks edgily. 'What? You must be joking!' Her face is blank with shock. Dad uncrumples himself and sits up, taking an interest again, as Mum continues to splutter down the telephone.

'But . . . ? What? What do you mean, there's nothing you can do? I thought you were a flipping travel agent?' More babbling. 'I'm not being abusive . . . What? Oh, for goodness sake! . . . Hello? Hello?' She slams down the phone and screams, 'Blooming useless!' at it as if the phone is defective in some way and that's why the holiday has all gone pear-shaped. My breath escapes in a long, sad sigh. There's no point in holding it any longer. It's blatantly obvious: the holiday's off.

'We need passports,' she explains unnecessarily, glaring at Dad like she's holding him personally responsible. 'And you flaming well haven't got one, have you?'

Then she looks at me and her face softens. 'Neither have you, sweetheart. We'll have to get you one.'

'Can we go then?' I ask, daring to hope.

Mum shakes her head regretfully. 'Not on that

holiday. We can't get them in time. It's my fault, I should have thought . . .'

'Never mind!' says Dad magnanimously. He plucks his wallet out of her hands and tucks the credit card safely back in, before stuffing it in his back pocket. 'Obviously wasn't meant to be. Shame.'

He looks remarkably light-hearted considering his disappointment.

'No,' says Mum sourly. 'Not this time maybe. But next time we'll be better prepared. Tomorrow morning, Martin Pottery, you get down that post office fast as you can and get yourself a passport form.'

Poor Mum. Poor me. We're the only ones who are really disappointed, you can tell. Even Grandma looks relieved.

'It was a bit impulsive, Jo, you've got to admit,' she says.

'Yeah, well next time I'll plan it properly,' says Mum, giving her a sour look.

The next day she doesn't wait for Dad, she goes straight out to collect the forms herself. Wise move. But then she discovers there's not enough time to send them off and get them back before Dad has to go back to work and she's furious. She blames him, of course.

'It's all your fault!'

'How d'you work that one out?' he asks, mystified. I must admit, I'm a bit perplexed too.

'You never wanted to go away in the first place!'

'Yes I did!' he lies, safe in the knowledge he's not going anywhere. Not till he gets a passport, anyway.

She's not going to let him wriggle out of this one

though. Straight away she makes us sit down and fill in the forms. Me and Dad, that is. She's got a passport already. Even though she's never used it since she met Dad, she's renewed it in the hope that one day she could force him, kicking and screaming, on an exotic foreign holiday. Some hope! Ezzie's got one too, all lined up for her big trip that's not going to happen. Ironic or what?

After that, Mum makes us go and have our photos taken and we're not allowed to smile. We look alike, two solemn mugshots staring blankly into the camera, each with fuzzy hair, though Dad's is cropped short. I look gross and Dad looks scary. Then she whips them off us anyway and takes them to the vicar who christened me but hasn't laid eyes on me or Dad since and bullies him into signing that he knows us really, really well. I didn't think that vicars were allowed to tell lies.

Finally, she produces my birth certificate, stuffs it with the form into the envelope and tells Dad to do the same.

And that's when the trouble starts.

Dad can't find his birth certificate.

'You must have it somewhere!' says Mum in exasperation, after we've hunted high and low all over the house. 'You'll have used it before!'

'When?' asks Dad. 'I don't think I've ever seen it!'

'When we got married! Didn't you need it then?'

'I can't remember,' says Dad, looking baffled. 'I don't think so.'

'Well, you weren't just wafted here from paradise, that's for sure,' says Mum suspiciously. 'You're doing this on purpose, aren't you?'

'No!' says Dad, and for once I believe him. 'I haven't got a clue where it is.'

'Round Grandma's,' says Ezzie, practical as ever. 'That's where it'll be. Grandma will have it tucked away somewhere safe.'

'Now why didn't I think of that?' says Mum, looking relieved. 'Martin, go round your mother's this minute and get that certificate.'

'I'm not a little kid you know!' grumbles Dad, but he picks up his keys and does as he's told. 'Coming, Flick?'

'Have you hidden it?' I ask, when we get in the car.

He grins. 'Not yet. But I will when I find it.'

He's joking.

I think.

'Why don't you want to go on holiday, Dad?'

'I do. I just don't particularly want to go abroad.' He swings the car expertly out into the slow stream of traffic.

'Why not?'

He shrugs. 'I don't know. Strange food. Foreign

language. Too hot. No real ale . . . Why would I want to go somewhere like that?'

''Cos it's different.'

A boy is loping along the pavement towards us, tall and skinny, hands in his pockets, dreadlocks down past his shoulders. I glance sideways at Dad and see a scowl forming on his face. It's Spud, on his way to our house. He raises his hand hesitantly as we pass and I wave back but Dad barely acknowledges him in return.

It strikes me that Dad doesn't do different.

When we get to Grandma's, she's out shopping but Grandpa's in the back garden, digging over his vegetable patch.

'What do you want me to plant this year, Flick?' he asks, resting his arms on the top of his spade. 'Courgettes? Cabbage? Nice bit of broccoli?'

Hmm.

*Would you rather eat courgettes or cabbage?*

Nice choice, Grandpa. How about pizza and chips? Now that's more like it.

'Anything, Gramps. They're all nice.' I wonder how many times I lie in the course of a day to save people's feelings.

'I'll see if I've got some sprouts to go in as well then. I know you're partial to them.'

Am I? Serves me right for telling porkies.

'Dad, Jo wants my birth certificate for the passport,' says Dad.

'What's that?' says Grandpa, who's disappeared into the shed on a sprout hunt. He's a bit hard of hearing, though he won't admit it.

'Where does Mum keep all her official stuff?' asks Dad, upping the decibel level. 'Certificates and that?'

'In the bureau, top shelf,' says Grandpa. I lean on the door and watch him. He's busy sifting through the pile of small brown envelopes marked up with his tiny, meticulous handwriting where he keeps his seeds. 'Key's in the kitchen drawer. Now then, what have we got here? Radishes, runner beans, squash, tomatoes . . . These are supposed to be in alphabetical order. Where did I put those sprouts?'

I love it in Grandpa's shed. It's crammed, top to toe, with things I never, ever, come into contact with in my world.

A row of long-handled spades, rakes, hoes and other gardening tools I don't know the name of take up the whole length of one wall, alongside three lawnmowers in various stages of disrepair; sacks of peat, compost, bone-meal and fertilizer spill their earthy contents on to the floor; old bikes, unused for years, pine away, yearning for long-lost summer days, alongside broken garden chairs, an ancient surfboard and a kite that has lost its strings; shelves groan under the weight of half-empty tins, inside which the remnants of paint, varnish, grout, stripper and something mysterious labelled 'sugar soap' fester away unnoticed; and jars of screws, nuts, bolts and paintbrushes wait patiently amongst balls of string and a bowl of curtain hooks, never to be used again.

Stacks of canes stand in corners along with odd pieces of wood which take on a scarily human appearance, draped as they are in old hats, anoraks and overalls. On the floor are rose-spouted watering cans, a hose, coiled like a cobra and, next to it, a smaller, viper-like curl of rope. Wellington boots stand to attention next to an armoury of trowels, shears, spades, forks, secateurs and muddy gardening gloves with holes in the fingers, assembled in a bucket, ready for action.

And beneath it all, the floorboards are strewn with wood shavings from Grandpa's lathe in the corner and the tang of the wood rises up to greet me as I stand by the door, and mingles with the earthy smell of fertilizer, peat, compost and bone-meal to produce a familiar, rich, smoky aroma that I think should be bottled and labelled 'Grandpa!' and sold for Christmas to all those kids who are not lucky enough to have a granddad like mine.

'Found them!' says Grandpa and holds the envelope aloft in triumph. 'I knew they were here somewhere. Where's your dad got to?'

'He's gone to look for his birth certificate,' I remind him.

'Birth certificate!' he says with a jolt. 'What does he want that for?'

'His passport.'

'Ah yes. Right then. I see.' He seems flustered.

'Anything the matter, Gramps?'

'No, no, nothing at all. Come on then, we'd better see how he's getting on.'

As we go in through the back door, knocking the soil from our boots, Grandma is coming through the front, her bags laden with shopping.

'Hello, darling!' she calls, catching sight of me. 'I must've known you were coming. I've just bought your favourite biscuits. Are you on your own?'

'Dad's here, somewhere,' I say and plant a kiss on her cheek. She smells as usual of Pears soap and Ponds cold cream. 'Here, give me those,' I say, reaching for the bags. 'Mmm, choccy biccies!'

'I'll put the kettle on,' says Gran.

'We haven't got time for a cup of tea,' says Dad, barging suddenly out of the sitting-room door. 'We've got to get a move on.'

'What's the hurry?' asks Grandma in surprise. 'You haven't even said hello yet.'

'Things to do,' he says, tucking something away into the inside pocket of his jacket. 'Sorry, must go. Come on, Flick.' He shoulders his way past her and disappears out of the front door without another word.

I stare after him, astonished. It's not like Dad to be so rude. He hasn't even looked at Grandma once. I find myself making excuses for him.

'Don't mind him, Grandma. He's in a rush to send off for his passport. He just dropped by to collect his birth certificate.'

Grandma turns towards Grandpa. She looks stunned. Grandpa shrugs imperceptibly and turns away into the sitting room, but not before I see the sadness in his eyes.

I'm really angry with my dad.

'Don't worry, Gran, I'll sort him out,' I say jokingly, but my attempt at humour falls on deaf ears. Grandma has already followed Grandpa into the sitting room and closed the door behind her.

Charming! They say teenagers have no manners but, I'm telling you, adults are a lot worse.

Next it's my turn to be a brat. I come home one day, late and grumpy, because Amy made me hang around after school with Mitch and his mates just in case they could be bothered to talk to us, but they're too busy play-fighting like little kids to notice we're there. Boys of that age can be so annoying. I hate being ignored at the best of times and this is bordering on humiliation.

I'm starving hungry and everyone's already eaten and my spaghetti bolognese has been left congealing on a plate and I've got loads of homework to do that night and I'm NOT in a good mood!

'There's a letter here for you,' says Mum, handing me a white envelope.

'In a minute!' I grunt and bung my dinner in the microwave without bothering to take it from her hand. Like there's any point? I know exactly what it's about. School is in the middle of sending out reminders about uniform and lateness and not going on holiday in term-time. Some hope!

I grab a can from the fridge and snap it open, spurting cola all over my shirt which adds to my strop, especially when I hear a snigger from Dad which he quickly turns into a cough. When the microwave pings I bang my plate and can on to a tray and say icily, 'I'm going in the other room to watch telly,' meaning, 'Don't anybody come near me or else!' The letter lies ignored on the worktop. From the corner of my eye I spot Ezzie smirking at Mum which is mega-annoying when you know you're acting out the teen version of a toddler in a tantrum but you can't stop.

In the lounge, I reach for the handset to switch on the telly and the tray slips sideways. My spag bol makes a bid for the floor and, luckily, I grab it just in time but, unluckily, this makes the can tip over and flood my dinner in cola. A scream of frustration rises in my throat.

Then I notice Mum and Dad and Ezzie have followed me in and are standing there together, watching me, with identical, creepy grins plastered over their faces like they've just stepped out of some weird horror movie.

'WHAT?' I ask in my best glacial tones.

Mum steps forward and takes the tray from my knee. Ezzie sits down next to me and hands me the envelope.

'We thought this might be important.'

I stare at it puzzled. It's franked with a logo which includes the words 'BBC Television'. My eyes open wide and my frosty voice melts to a soft whisper.

'What is it?'

Ezzie leans forward conspiratorially and whispers back, 'Open it and see.'

I stare up at my parents and gulp. They nod, quickly and simultaneously, my father with his arms folded, my mother biting her nails.

'Go on,' Mum says. 'Open it.'

'It's probably nothing.' I turn it over and over in my hands. 'It's probably an acknowledgement or something . . . It's probably just a—'

'OPEN it!' orders Dad.

I do as I'm told.

THEN I SCREAM MY FLIPPING HEAD OFF!!!!!!!!

We end up having a party! Dad cracks open a bottle of sparkling wine left over from Christmas, and does that thing where you shake the bottle and it spurts out, like they do on the motor racing on the telly. It goes everywhere, all over the sofa and the carpet and us as well, but Mum just laughs and says, 'Save us some!' and he pours us each a glass. Ezzie says, 'Better not,' and pats her tummy and, for a split second, Dad looks sad, then he says, 'Just a drop,' and pours a minuscule amount into another glass and thrusts it into her hand. 'Put hairs on his chest, that will,' he says and then he pats her tummy too and she smiles at him. I can feel myself filling up, honest I can. Then all of a sudden, Spud arrives, and Dad surprises us all, especially Spud, by handing him the spare glass of bubbly.

Then Dad decides to make a night of it and go out and get us all takeaway and pick up a few cans at the same time. Well, I haven't eaten and neither has Spud who now seems to be included in the jollification and, even though everyone else has, they all agree it's a celebration and, what the hell, they could always manage some more. And Spud, made bold by an unexpected glass of fizzy wine, says, 'Wanna hand?' and Dad says, 'Aye, OK then,' and they go off together like old mates, even though Spud still looks a bit wary, which is understandable since this is the first time Dad has ever treated him remotely like a person.

As soon as they've gone, Mum phones Grandpa and Grandma to tell them the good news which, in case you haven't guessed yet, is that I have been chosen as one of the four finalists in the competition. I have to go to the Television Studios in London and read my piece *before camera*! And they're so excited they come over immediately and they bring with them a bottle of *real* champagne. This time we open it sensibly and Grandpa proposes a toast, 'To Flick!' and we all chink our glasses together and sip our drinks. It's nice and sweet and makes me feel warm inside but, to tell the truth, it's wasted on me. I can't tell the difference between the real stuff and the cheap plonk.

'I knew you'd do it!' Gran keeps saying. 'I knew you'd win!'

When Dad and Spud come back, laden with strong-smelling, brown paper bags full of Chinese food and a carton of beer, Grandma looks a bit cross to see Spud. Actually, I can't help noticing, Dad looks a bit cross to see *her*, and Mum must have thought so too because she takes the bags off him and whispers, 'Don't worry, there's plenty to go round. You've got enough here to feed an army!'

But I don't think that's the reason Dad looks put out. He's been funny with Grandma and Grandpa since the day we went round to look for his birth certificate.

Anyway, tonight he makes an effort and offers them some Chinese and Grandpa says, 'Don't mind if I do,' and helps himself and soon it's like old times, with us all sitting around tucking into piled-up plates of yummy food and Dad and Gramps laying into the beer. Dad offers Spud a can and at first he refuses but my father won't take no for an answer, so in the end he accepts he's beaten and takes one in good grace.

'You're not a drinker, Spud?' observes Mum kindly.

'Not really.'

'Spud likes natural things. Water, juices . . .' says Ezzie.

'Beer's natural,' says Dad and takes a long swig of his. 'It's made from hops. Can't get more natural than that.'

'Not this stuff,' says Grandpa gloomily, inspecting the can. 'It's full of chemicals.'

'I've got some orange juice in the fridge,' Mum offers. 'Flick, go and fetch Spud some of that orange juice.'

Spud shakes his head and opens the can. 'This is fine, honest.' He holds it up to me in homage and takes a sip. 'Special occasion, innit?'

'He doesn't like beef or pork or prawns neither,' Dad remarks, waving his fork at Spud. 'Here, you should've seen him trying to pick something he could eat off the menu. He's a blooming nightmare.' His words are derisive, but the tone is affectionate.

Spud doesn't seem to mind. He carries on quietly tucking into his noodles.

'Are you vegetarian, Spud?' asks Mum.

'I try to be.'

'Best thing for you, vegetables,' declares Grandpa.

'You should see Grandpa's vegetable plot,' says Mum. 'He grows everything in it. Spinach, beetroot, carrots . . .'

'Raspberries, strawberries, blueberries . . .' I chip in.

'Blueberries!' says Spud in admiration. 'I never had much success with them.'

'Don't rush them,' says Grandpa. 'They like to take their time. They like acid soil too. Give 'em plenty of moisture and they'll come.'

'Right,' says Spud. 'I'll remember that.'

'Spud's got his own allotment,' explains Ezzie. 'Up by the college.'

'Have you?' says Grandpa with interest. 'What you got on it?'

'I started with potatoes. Then I tried courgettes, onions, peas, the usual stuff ... '

'Is that why they call you Spud?' interrupts Dad and laughs loudly at his own joke, mouth wide open. Not a good look when you're in the middle of eating a Chinese banquet.

'Yeah, 'course,' says Spud quietly, not in the least put out. 'Why else? I mean I'm not exactly a King Edward, am I?'

'That's what Dad said,' I say in surprise. Dad gives me a dirty look then stares at Spud as if he's suddenly discovered he's got more to him than meets the eye.

'What's your real name?' I ask as it occurs to me for the first time that he probably wasn't christened Spud.

'Alastair,' he says. 'Alastair Fernley-Jones.'

We all stare at Alastair Fernley-Jones with his rope-like

coils of matted hair, piercings, scruffy jeans and faded T-shirt. He forks a pile of bean sprouts into his mouth, unconcerned by our scrutiny.

'I prefer Spud,' he says, indistinctly.

'Yeah,' I say, voicing, I'm pretty sure, everyone's opinion. 'Suits you.'

'Wonder what you'll have to do in London, Flick?' asks Ezzie, changing the subject.

'Say my piece to camera, it says in the letter.'

'D'you get to stay the night?'

'Yeah, in a posh hotel.'

'Lucky!' she says wistfully. 'Who's going with you?'

'Me!' say Mum and Dad simultaneously. Everyone laughs.

'Only one of you can come,' I say, remembering the conditions. 'Then, if I win, one of you accompanies me abroad somewhere.' Excitement grips my stomach.

Mum sits up, alert. 'Actually, we do need to think this through properly, Martin.'

'Sorted. I'll take her to London, you take her abroad.'

'But what if she doesn't—' Mum breaks off as she realizes, too late, what she's about to say.

I say it for her. 'I won't win. You might as well come with me to London, Mum.'

'Yes you will,' says Gran, who's been uncharacteristically quiet throughout the evening. She falls into her usual patter. 'Clever girl like you, you'll win all right. She's just like her Aunty Libby, isn't she, Bert?'

Dad scowls. 'No she's not,' he says churlishly. 'She's like herself!'

Everyone looks surprised and Grandma shrinks back into herself as if he's smacked her in the face.

'Martin!' says Mum reprovingly. 'That's no way to talk to your mother!'

'Well, it gets on my nerves, her going on all the time,' he says bitterly. '*Just like her Aunty Libby!* She thinks Flick being clever is something to do with her, that it's been passed on through the family.'

'Martin, stop it!' says Mum, horrified.

'I didn't mean that,' says Grandma, distressed.

'No, because it doesn't work like that, does it?' He thrusts his face belligerently at Grandma. 'I may not be the brightest fairy light on the Christmas tree. But my daughters are, so there! Flick and Ezzie, both of them. And it's nothing to do with you or Libby or anyone else in this family, is it?'

He doesn't sound like a grown man. He sounds like a little kid in a strop, going '*Nah, nah, nah, nah, nah,*' to his parents because they've upset him.

'Come on, Lizzie love, it's time we made a move.' Grandpa's voice is sensible and grown up, in direct contrast to Dad's. He helps Grandma up out of the chair. Mum fetches her coat and places it round her shoulders.

'I'm sorry,' she says, looking daggers at Dad. 'I don't know what's got into him.'

Gran pats her hand and nods. Her face is white.

'Goodnight, everyone,' she says quietly and we all chorus, 'Night, night.'

All of us, except Dad.

Grandma pauses but he ignores her, raising his can defiantly and pouring what's left of it down his throat. Grandpa shakes his head in disgust and ushers her gently outside. I shiver in the cold night air that finds its way through the open front door as Mum follows them out to the car, her voice rising and falling, apologetic and placatory. After a while, I hear the car drive off and the front door slams.

Spud clears his throat and stands up. 'I'd better make a move myself, Ez,' he says. Ezzie nods and he bends and plants a kiss on her cheek. 'I'll see myself out. Thanks for the food and drink, Mr Pottery.'

'Aye,' says Dad, putting his can back down on the table. He wipes his mouth with the back of his hand. 'See you again, Spud,' he says pleasantly, as if nothing's happened.

'Night, Mrs Pottery.' Spud sidles past Mum who's appeared at the kitchen door, eyes blazing.

'He may be cabbage-looking but he's not as green as

he makes out, that lad,' says Dad conversationally as the door closes behind Spud.

Mum glares at him, her hands on his hips. 'Do you mind telling me what all that was about?' she demands.

Dad sighs. 'I'm sorry about that.'

'It's not me you should be apologizing to. It's your mother. How dare you speak to her like that?'

Dad has the grace to look ashamed.

'She was asking for it.'

'Asking for what?'

'Telling our Flick she's like Libby. Going on and on about Libby all the time, like she's Brain of Britain or something. It gets on my nerves.'

'She's proud of her, Martin. She's her daughter. She's proud of Flick too. What's wrong with that?'

Is Dad jealous of Aunty Libby? Is that what all this is about? The same thought must have occurred to Mum because she adds, more gently this time, 'She's proud of you as well, you know.'

Dad shakes his head impatiently.

'She's an old woman, Martin. She thinks the world of you, the girls, all of us. They both do.'

'That's what you think!' Dad's voice is bitter again.

Mum clicks her tongue in disgust and turns away from him. 'Now you're being ridiculous. I don't know what's got into you, Martin.' She starts to clear the table, clashing the plates together angrily. 'She loves you, for goodness sake. Show her some respect. She's your mother.'

'No, she's not.'

Mum stops crashing plates. 'What did you say?'

'She's *not* my mother.'

'What do you mean? You can't ditch her because she gets on your nerves.' She gives a little nervous giggle. 'Most people would disown their mothers in that case. I know I would.'

Dad's voice drops to a whisper.

'She's not my birth mother.'

Dad says these words quietly but he might as well have shouted them from the rooftops, the effect it has on us all. A plate slips from Mum's hand on to the table with a loud clatter. Ezzie turns to me with a puzzled frown and automatically I slide my hand into hers. She grips it tight.

Mum sits down heavily next to Dad at the table. 'My goodness. Where has all this come from?'

Dad shakes his head like he doesn't trust himself to speak.

'Are you sure?' Mum asks softly.

He laughs bitterly. 'Oh yeah, I'm sure all right. I've got the certificate to prove it.'

'What do you mean?'

He stares into the distance, lost in a world of his own. Mum lays her hand on his arm, confused, and he blinks and comes to, putting his arm around her and hugging her tight. I bite my lip and edge closer to Ezzie.

'I can't take this in,' says Mum. 'When did you find out?'

Dad gives a big sigh and lets her go. 'Remember the other day I went over to look for my birth certificate? Well, I found it all right. Only it turned out to be an adoption certificate. It had my name on it and the date the adoption was granted and the names, Elizabeth and Albert Pottery. Adoptive parents.'

My dad's found out he was adopted! I *knew* there was something wrong that day!

Mum shakes her head in disbelief. 'And they never told you?'

'Not a sausage. They've kept it a secret all this time. I'd probably never have found out if I hadn't gone looking for my birth certificate.' He looks angry. 'I had a right to know, Jo. But they never said a word.'

'Mum?' They turn to look at us, almost surprised, as if they've forgotten we're there. 'Dad?' My voice is tiny, like I'm scared to ask the question in case I don't like the answer. 'Does this mean that Grandma and Grandpa aren't our real grandparents?'

'Don't be daft!' says Mum. 'Of course they are! Come here, you big wally!' She crushes me in her arms and relief courses through me. 'You mean everything to them, you girls, you don't need me to tell you that.'

I love my mum. She does go on a bit but she always

makes things right. But Dad still looks upset and Mum adds, 'And so do you! You're their son, Martin, whether they adopted you or conceived you themselves.'

Dad shakes his head.

'Yes you are, you idiot! Who were the ones who fed you, changed you, sat up with you through the night when you were ill? Who were the ones who wiped your snotty nose, bandaged your knees, mopped up your tears? Who were the ones who—'

'It's not the same,' says Dad, cutting her short in full flow. A closed, stubborn look comes down over his face.

'Of course it is!' says Mum, working herself up into a fury. 'Listen to me, you big dope! Grandma Liz was a proper mother to you, not like the stupid woman who gave birth to you. Any fool can get themselves pregnant, have a baby, then walk away from their responsibilities . . .'

Ezzie gasps and runs out of the room.

'Oh no!' Mum claps her hand to her mouth, horrified. 'Me and my big mouth! Why didn't you stop me? Ezzie!'

She dashes upstairs after her, shouting, 'Ezzie! I'm sorry, darling! I didn't mean you . . . Ezzie? Ezzie!'

A door slams shut upstairs followed by muted sobbing. We can hear Mum hammering and pleading, 'Ezzie? Let me in, darling! Ezzie, please? Listen to me, sweetheart!'

Dad and I stare at each other morosely.

'Oops!' he says. 'Your mother, hey?'

'Jumps in with both feet,' I agree.

'Least it got her off my back,' he says with an ironic, twisted grin.

I go and sit on his knee, folding my arms around his neck. His arms encircle me protectively and I snuggle in close to his chest, like a little kid.

From upstairs the sobbing recedes. We hear the door being unlocked and Ezzie saying, 'Oh, Mum . . .' followed by the low sound of murmuring.

'Girls, girls, girls,' Dad says and strokes my hair. I feel his heart beating, slow and steady as the clock on the mantelpiece. I wonder if Ezzie's baby is listening to her mum's heart beating, keeping her safe, ticking away the hours till she's ready to be born.

I bet it's a girl.

After a bit, Dad says, 'Time to put the kettle on, hey? Think we could all do with a cuppa.'

I gaze up at him, loath to let him go. Then I say:

*'Would you rather . . . have a cup of tea or another hug from me?'*

'A cup of tea or another hug from you. Mmm.' He pretends to consider. 'Cup of tea, please. And a chocolate biscuit!'

'Cheek!' But my arms release him and I get up to fill

the kettle. The water spurts out from the tap and splatters against the spout of the kettle, soaking me. I swear loudly.

Dad laughs. 'Language! Don't let your mother hear you!'

'Hear what?' Mum's standing at the door.

'Ezzie all right?' asks Dad softly.

Mum nods. 'She is now. She's having a bit of a lie-down.' She sits down heavily at the table. 'Me and my big mouth!'

'You were right though. As usual.' He sits down next to her. 'I owe my mother an apology. I shouldn't have had a go at her. It's not her fault.' He sighs deeply. 'Though I can't understand why they've never told me I was adopted.'

'What did they say when you found the certificate?'

'Nothing. We haven't talked about it.'

'You're kidding!'

'They know I've found out though.'

'They do now! You need to talk, Martin. They've thought of you as theirs all those years . . . It must be so hard for them now you've discovered the truth.'

'I suppose so. I reckon they thought I'd never find out. It's like they'd forgotten they'd adopted me in the first place.' Dad hesitates, then he adds quietly, 'I wonder if *she's* forgotten too.'

'Who?'

'My real mother.' His face darkens.

Mum covers his hand with hers. 'I was stupid to say what I did earlier. She . . . your birth mother . . . must have had a good reason to put you up for adoption. It can't have been easy to give you away.'

He shakes her hand away impatiently. 'You reckon? Come on, Jo, she didn't want me, that's the truth of it.'

'Don't be daft!' says Mum, but her eyes are round with concern. 'Nothing's ever that simple.'

'Yes it is,' says Dad bitterly. 'I wasn't planned and I was an inconvenience. End of story.'

'You don't know that!'

'Of course I do. It's obvious. I would have ruined her life so she got rid of me.'

'Look, Martin,' says Mum sounding distressed, 'I know you're angry and I don't blame you . . .'

'Angry?' says Dad. 'I'm not angry!' But I don't believe him. 'What have I got to be angry about? I've had a good life. The only thing that bugs me is the fact that I didn't know.' He stands up decisively and shoves his chair firmly under the table. 'Anyway, I'm going out for a walk,' he announces. 'Clear my head.'

'Good idea,' says Mum quietly but he doesn't look at her.

'Best thing all round, adoption,' he says, his voice sounding empty and flat. 'Maybe our Ezzie should consider it.'

He walks out of the door.

Everything falls silent.

The clock ticks on, slowly, relentlessly.

*Would you rather . . . keep your baby or have it adopted? Keep your baby or have it adopted? Keep your baby or have it adopted . . . ?*

'Mum?' I ask, my voice small with fear. 'Ezzie's not going to have *her* baby adopted, is she?'

Mum looks stricken.

'I don't think so, Flick,' she says. 'But at the end of the day, it's Ezzie's baby and it's her choice.'

Amy is so over the moon, you'd swear she'd won the competition herself.

'You're going to be on the telly!' she squeals.

'Only if I get through the next round,' I correct her.

'I thought you had to do a piece to camera?'

'That's just for them to choose the winner. There's four of us, remember. They're going to put our articles on autocue and then we have to read them aloud while they film us. Then they play them back and decide which one of us they're going to choose to report on some big event for children's television.'

'You'll win, I know you will!' She sounds like Grandma.

'I know I won't,' I mutter. I've got butterflies now, to tell the truth. I mean, it's one thing bashing out 800 words on your old computer; it's another thing reading them live on camera to television people. They're not going to be interested in a school footie match, are they?

Amy doesn't seem to share any of my concerns. She's getting carried away as usual.

'Flick, it's fantastic. You'll be a celeb! You'll be in all the mags! You'll have your own designer range of clothes! You'll have a perfume named after you and you'll probably get a modelling contract and . . .'

'It's not like that, stupid!' I protest. 'It's journalism, not *The X Factor*. Anyway, I won't get through.'

'Yes you will. When will you find out? On the day?'

'I'm not sure.'

'Oh, it's going to be so exciting! I wish I was coming with you!' she says wistfully, her face pinched with longing.

'I do too,' I say untruthfully. Amy would do my head in; I need someone to calm me down, not wind me up like a coiled spring.

'What are you going to wear?'

'I don't know. I haven't got anything.'

'No, you haven't, have you?' Sympathetic, but hardly comforting. 'You've got to make an impression, Flick. You can borrow something of mine if you want. How about my white sparkly top with the cutaway back and my skin-tight jeans? Only with your legs you'll need really high shoes or the jeans'll be too long.'

Thanks, Amy, for reminding me of my short stumpy

legs. I'm not sure I want to make the sort of impression she's talking about anyway. Her sparkly top is *so* tarty.

'It's OK, I'll find something. I don't know if I want to go really dressed up.'

She's not going to give up that easily. If she can't go on the telly, she's determined her clothes will.

'Come on, Flick. This is your big chance. Listen, what about my metallic dress, with the studded belt? Or my new mini-dress with your black leather boots? That would look stunning!'

Hmm. Nice choice, Amy.

*Would you rather a shimmering silver metallic dress with plunging neckline that will reveal your undeveloped boobs, or a green ruffled mini that will show off your undeveloped legs?*

No, come to think of it, that hideous mini-dress of Amy's would cover my short stumps anyway. I could tuck it into my black leather boots, get myself a bow and arrow and pretend I'm a vertically-challenged Robin Hood.

My heart plummets. I wish I'd never started this in the first place. I had no idea it would turn out to be so complicated.

Mum and Dad have had an argument about who's

going to chaperone me to London. Dad wanted to take me because he said if I win, he doesn't want to go abroad anyway.

Then Mum said narkily, 'Yes, but if she doesn't, I don't get to go anywhere, do I? And that's not fair, because I'm the one who wants to go away, not you.'

'You couldn't drive her to London!' said Dad scornfully. 'You know what you're like!' and Mum said, 'What? What am I like?' and soon they were seriously going at it, hammer and tongs, until Ezzie chipped in with, 'Just listen to you two! It's not about you anyway. If anyone should go it should be Grandma because she's the one who encourages her.'

Mum looked a bit embarrassed then and Dad looked a bit put out and they both got the huff and pretended they didn't care who went anyway. Finally, when they'd calmed down, it was decided that Mum would take me on the train, because she's best if I get nervous and she'd be good at helping me get ready whereas Dad wouldn't have a clue.

Plus, it was blatantly obvious she would bite her right arm off to stay a night in a swanky hotel.

Funny thing was, no one thought of asking me who I wanted to come with me.

I suppose I would've chosen Mum anyway. But Ezzie was right. It was Grandma who deserved it.

But the thing is, I feel a little bit weird about my grandparents now. Because they're not actually, are they? My grandparents, I mean. Not any more. Not since we found out Dad was adopted. It's fine Mum going on about how much they love us, I know they do. And I love them to bits too. But the thing is, I know how Dad feels. They're not my flesh and blood any more. It's not the same.

I feel like I'm a link in a chain that has been broken and mended. Only most of the links that used to be there are missing now. It's made it into something different; something shorter. A bracelet instead of a necklace.

I preferred the necklace.

Nobody's talking about it. The adoption, I mean.

Do you know, I don't even think Grandma and Grandpa are aware that Ezzie and I know Dad was adopted. They probably think because he hasn't spoken to them about it, he hasn't told us either. It's obvious to them *he* knows because, let's face it, they saw him go off with the certificate and then witnessed his little outburst the next time they met up. They haven't mentioned it though. When you've kept a secret for so long, it's probably easier to brush the truth back under the carpet where it's been hidden for the past forty years.

'You want to go round there and talk to them!' said Mum, but Dad shook his head.

'What good would that do?'

'Don't you want to find out about your birth mother?' asked Mum.

'She gave me away,' he said bluntly. 'End of story. What more is there to find out? Anyway,' he continued, 'you were right. These are my parents, Liz and Bert, the people who brought me up. It was a long time ago. No point in raking over old ground.'

Mum opened her mouth to protest but Dad said, 'End of subject!' and she closed it again.

But personally, I don't think Dad was being entirely honest with himself. Because I remember him saying, 'I had a right to know, Jo,' and looking really upset the night it all came out.

Ez and I go round for tea at Grandma's the night before my audition. Mum said they wanted to see me before my trip.

'All ready then?' asks Grandpa.

Ezzie laughs. 'Flick is. Mum's still packing. She keeps trying on clothes and putting them in her bag then taking them all out again. You'd swear she was the one who was having a screen test, not Flick.'

Grandma chuckles. 'She's excited . . . and I don't blame her.' She ladles huge helpings of chicken casserole on to our plates and when we protest she says to me, 'You need all your strength if you're off to London,' as if I'm actually going on a solo trek to the North Pole, and then she turns to Ezzie and says, 'and you're eating for two!'

Grandpa says, 'Bossy madam, isn't she? Better get stuck in or she'll be after us with a broom.' Sometimes I think Grandpa believes we're still about six years old. Still, we tuck into our steaming plates of chicken and veg obediently, mopping it up with big chunks of crusty loaf. That's a habit left over from our childhood too. Grandpa always told me I had to wipe my plate clean because Grandma didn't like washing up. I believed him for years.

After we've dutifully cleared our plates, Grandma brings out a home-made apple pie with a dish of clotted cream and we all groan but nobody refuses a piece. What are my grandparents like, with their home-grown vegetables and wholesome cooking? It strikes me that Grandma has spent her whole life doing this, providing tasty, nourishing meals for her family.

'Did you ever have a job, Grandma?' I ask, sitting back, full as a gug. Amy once asked me, 'What's a gug?' after we'd had tea at our house and my dad said he was full as one.

'Blowed if I know,' he'd said, scratching his head. 'It's just one of those things we've always said in our family.'

I guess all families have sayings of their own.

'I certainly did,' says Grandma. 'When I left school I went to work in an office. I was there for years.'

'What sort of office?'

'It was an accountancy firm. I was secretary to the boss.'

'A very good job it was too,' says Grandpa, pushing away his empty bowl with a small belch of pleasure.

'Pardon me. She was a very clever young lady, your grandma. She could have gone to university.'

'Could you?' remarks Ezzie with interest.

Grandma snorts. 'Don't listen to him. How could I go to university? I was the oldest and my father had recently died. I had to go out and earn a living and bring my wages home to my mother. She had eight mouths to feed. That's the way it was in those days.'

'When did you give up work?' I ask.

'When I found out I was expecting your Aunty Libby. You had to in those days, there was no employment protection then.' She sounds regretful.

'Would you have liked to carry on?'

'Oh aye,' says Grandma. 'It was a lovely job.'

'They were that sorry when she left,' remarks Grandpa. 'They wanted to make her office manager.'

'I'd like to have gone to university too,' she adds wistfully.

How strange. I'd never thought about Grandma as a young woman with a career and ambitions of her own. I thought she just had them for us. 'Have you got any photographs from that time, Grandma?'

'I expect so. I'll just clear the table and then we'll have a look.'

'We'll do that,' says Ezzie, taking charge. 'You find the photos.'

'She used to run that office for them,' Grandpa recalls as he bends down and rummages through the sideboard. 'Now then, what have we got here?' He pulls out some old photo albums and straightens up with a groan. 'Years since I looked through these things.'

By the time Ezzie and I have washed up and cleared away, Grandpa's put a stack of albums and cardboard boxes out on the table. We all sit around and go through them. Some of them are really old pictures, brown and cream in colour, of women in long dresses, nipped in at the waist, and mustachioed men in suits and waistcoats with watch chains.

'That was my mother,' says Grandma, pointing to a serious-looking young woman with large soft eyes, high cheekbones and bow-shaped lips, her hair pulled back severely behind her ears. 'She was a real beauty when she was young.'

'You're the spit of her, Ez!' I gasp. Ezzie studies her carefully, a puzzled frown on her face.

'Who do I look like then?' I ask, turning the pages.

'You don't need me to tell you that!' laughs Grandma. 'You take after your dad, anyone can see that.'

'Why did I have to inherit Dad's mushroom cloud?' I grumble.

'You remind me of my younger sister too,' says Grandma, turning the page. 'Our Maisie. She had straight

82

hair but she was little, like you, with the same arched eyebrows and enquiring eyes. Look, there she is, next to my brothers.' I peer at the minuscule picture before me but can see little resemblance without the halo of curls.

'What do you think, Ez? Reckon I look like her?'

Ezzie examines the photograph closely then stares at me. 'Yeah,' she says, like she's trying to puzzle it out. 'You do, a bit.'

'Poor thing,' I say. 'Have you got any of you when you were young, Grandma?'

We pore over the photos for hours, until they're scattered all over the table. Some of them I've seen before, though not for ages. There's one of Grandma as a girl, looking like Ezzie with her long hair tumbling over her shoulders, and there's a black and white studio picture of her as a young woman, smiling shyly into the camera. She's wearing a smart, fitted dress with a bold pattern and dark lipstick and her hair is shiny and sleek now, turning under gently at her shoulders and pinned back at the front in a large swirl.

'My twenty-first birthday,' she says wonderingly.

'You look lovely, Gran,' says Ezzie. 'That forties look is all the rage now.'

There's a wedding photo too, which I've seen before, very formal and serious. Grandpa's in uniform and Grandma's wearing a plain jacket with shoulder pads and a slimline skirt, a corsage of flowers in her buttonhole.

'Wartime,' she explains. 'No lovely white dresses for us. I had to save up my coupons for months to buy that outfit.'

'She looked beautiful,' says Grandpa. 'I was on leave. All I had was a weekend then they sent me back.'

'I didn't see him for another three months till the war ended,' agrees Grandma.

There's an album full of black and white photos of Aunty Libby as a baby, sitting up in her pram, a massive affair with huge wheels, then a school photograph of her sitting behind a desk, grinning into the camera. She's wearing a dress with a smocked front and a Peter Pan collar and a hand-knitted cardigan. Her hair is parted neatly to one side and fastened in a huge bow.

'I used to make all her clothes myself,' remarks Grandma softly. 'It was blue, that dress, with a white collar. I sat up all night, hand-smocking it, so it would be ready for the school photo. I knitted that cardigan too. As pretty as a picture she looked.'

'Literally,' I say and she smiles at me.

There are more of Aunty Libby, one, hand in hand with Grandpa, another with her arms round Grandma's neck, hugging her tight; there are loads of her on holiday in Blackpool, eating candy floss, having a ride on a donkey, posing in a rucked bathing-suit, waving at the camera. In all of them she's laughing, her eyes sparkling, her face alive with joy.

'She looks like fun!' I say approvingly.

'She was a happy little thing,' says Grandma, a little smile playing on her lips.

'Why doesn't she come home more often?' I wonder aloud. 'I can't remember ever seeing her.'

'She's busy,' says Grandma shortly, standing up beside me and snapping the album shut. 'She's got an important job, a husband and children to look after. She hasn't got time to come running down here to see us.'

'I hope I'm never too busy to come and see you, Grandma,' I say, snuggling into her.

'I hope so too,' she says. She sounds choked.

When I glance up at her, she looks like she's about to cry.

'That's enough for tonight,' says Grandpa, starting to gather up the loose photographs.

'What about Dad?' I say. 'We haven't seen any of him when he was little?'

'You've seen those before,' Grandma says, but she picks out an album and opens it up. 'Be quick then, or your mother will be telling me off.'

I flick through the album in front of me, glancing at the more familiar photos of Dad as a baby and a little boy. Funny how by the time you get to your teenage years, your parents stop taking photos of you. Dad was cute when he was little; stocky and round-faced.

'He looked like you when he was a baby, Gramps,' I say in surprise.

'Bald and chubby. I think you might be right there,' chuckles Grandpa.

'He didn't have a hair on his head till he was twelve months old,' remarks Grandma fondly. 'Just like you, Flick. It's often like that when you've got curly hair. It takes a long time growing.'

'That's because it's deformed,' says Ezzie. 'It's true,' she says indignantly when I give her a thump. 'We did it in human biology!'

'It's not fair,' I grumble. 'Nobody else has got deformed hair.'

'No,' says Ezzie thoughtfully.

'He is like you, Grandpa, look.' I point to a picture of Grandpa in shirt-sleeves and braces, holding Dad as a baby in his arms. 'You could be Dad there, if you had curly hair and different clothes on.'

'I was about the same age as he is now,' agrees Grandpa. 'That's why you see the resemblance.'

'You were quite old when you had Dad, weren't you?' I say, without thinking. There's an uncomfortable silence. I glance up to see Ezzie frowning at me and I feel myself going red.

All these family photographs . . . they'd made me forget I'm not supposed to know Dad had been adopted. Not as far as Grandma and Granddad are concerned. Big secret!

'Sorry,' I mumble. 'I didn't mean to be rude. I was just wondering why you decided to have him? After all that time, I mean. Like, why didn't you have him before . . . ?' My voice tails away miserably as I realize I'm being incredibly nosy and digging a bigger hole for myself with every word I utter. 'Sorry . . . it's none of my business . . .'

I feel awful. They must think I'm questioning them on their sex life!

Grandma sighs. 'We would have liked a bigger family, Flick, but it just didn't happen. We waited a long time for our Libby . . .'

'. . . and an even longer time for your dad,' finished Grandpa. 'And then we started all over again.'

Unspoken words hang heavy in the air. Ezzie practically crosses her eyes in desperation, warning me not to say any more. I'm not going to. I've said too much already and I feel like a right nosy parker.

Something has changed. It feels different somehow, sad. And it's my fault. I give a huge sigh.

*'Would you rather . . . ?'*

Three pairs of eyes look at me in surprise.

*'. . . have had loads of kids and no grandchildren or just
two kids and me and Ezzie?'*

'Two kids and you and Ezzie of course!' Grandma raps
out the correct answer without hesitation.

'That's all right then!' I beam at her happily. 'You've
got us now. Aren't you lucky?'

Grandpa bursts out laughing and leans over and ruffles
my hair. 'Here,' he says, digging into his back pocket and
pulling out a twenty-pound note. 'Before I forget. Take
this and buy yourself something nice in London.'

'Thanks, Grandpa!' I give him a hug and he says
gruffly, 'Best be off now, you've got a big day tomorrow.'

'Bye, Grandma!' I shout because she's disappeared into
the other room.

'Wait a minute,' she calls and then she's back, clutching
a paper bag in her hands. 'I've got something for you too.'

Inside is a lovely old writing book, with a rich blue
velvet cover, decorated with tiny gold and silver sequins.
The pages are formed from rich, creamy parchment and
there's a matching blue silk ribbon attached to use as a
marker. It looks as if it's come from a bygone age and it's
so special, I don't know what to say.

'Now you're a proper writer,' she says, 'you'll need a
nice book to write in.'

'It's beautiful, Grandma,' I say, finding my voice.

'It was mine,' she says softly. 'My father gave it to me just before he died. He said it was for when I went to university.'

I shake my head regretfully. 'You should keep it, Grandma. It's too good for me to use.'

'Nonsense!' she says emphatically. 'What's the point of a writing book if there's nothing in it? You're a good writer, aren't you? You've proved that. So you make good use of it.'

'I didn't know you'd kept that,' says Grandpa quietly.

'Always knew it would come in useful one day,' she smiles. 'Now then, Felicity Pottery. You make sure you write down everything that happens in London so I can read all about it when you get home.'

Ezzie is really quiet on the way home. I don't realize at first because I'm babbling on about my beautiful new book and how special it is and how I'm going to write down absolutely everything that happens to me in it so I won't forget a single bit of this amazing experience, blah, blah, blah . . . and then I notice she's not saying very much. Suddenly it hits me. I am being incredibly insensitive *again*. I stop short in my tracks and wail, 'I'm sorry . . . !'

Ezzie turns to look at me, startled. 'What are you sorry for now?'

'Going on like that. London. The book . . . everything . . .'

'What?' She frowns. 'What are you on about?'

'Don't you mind?'

'Mind?' She looks genuinely baffled. 'Why should I mind? I think it's great.'

'You don't mind Grandma giving me the book?' I say in a small voice.

She's looking at me as if I've taken leave of my senses. 'Why would I?'

'Only, I just thought . . . when she was going on about university and that . . .' My voice fades away.

'Flick? Spit it out, please!'

'. . . maybe she was keeping it for you when you started uni!' I say in a rush, my words bolting out like a sprinter from the starting block.

'Oh!' Ezzie considers my words. 'I don't think so. That hadn't even occurred to me. In that case,' she adds with a wry grin, 'just as well she gave it to you instead.'

'You really don't mind?'

'Of course not! How many times? You're not doing me out of my inheritance, Flick, it's only a flipping book. Nice as it is . . .' she adds hastily.

'That's all right then!' I grin back at her in relief. 'Phew! I thought I'd put my foot in it again.' I slip my arm through hers and we start walking again, in step. 'Why are you so quiet then?'

'I'm thinking.'

'What about?'

'Everything.'

I nod understandingly. 'You've got a lot to think about, with the baby and that.'

Ezzie is silent. 'Actually,' she says after a while, 'I was thinking about those photographs.'

'They were great, weren't they? Dad was so cute when he was a baby. No wonder they chose him. He looked just like Grandpa.'

'Don't you think that's a bit strange?'

'Nah. All babies look like Grandpa: round-faced, bald, not many teeth.'

'What about those other ones then? I looked like Grandma's mother, you said so yourself. And you looked a bit like her sister.'

'So?'

'Dad's adopted. So we're not related to these dead people. But we looked like them.'

I struggle to remember the photographs among the hundreds we'd looked at but they've merged into a creamy-brown haze. 'We probably didn't, Ez. Not really.'

'But you said I looked like Grandma's mother!'

'I know I did.' I try to remember the photograph. A girl wearing a dress with a high collar, staring solemnly into the camera. 'I'm not sure now though. I think I might have said it just to please Grandma.'

'You reckon?' Ezzie sounds disappointed.

'People do it all the time. They look for resemblances. They even do it with their pets! Remember how everyone used to say Buster had your eyes!'

'Yeah, they did!' Ezzie giggles. 'I wonder what this poor baby is going to look like? Buster's eyes and Spud's dreadlocks!'

'Dad'll have a fit!' I'm struck afresh with remorse. 'Oh, Ez, I can't believe I asked Grandma why she waited so long to have Dad!'

Ezzie grins in agreement. 'Bit personal, that!'

'I didn't mean it like that. I meant, why did they decide to adopt a baby after all that time? But I couldn't say that, could I? Being as we're not supposed to know anything about it.'

'They've probably worked out by now that we do.'

'I suppose so.' I sigh heavily. 'I wish it was out in the open and we could all talk about it properly.'

Ezzie shrugs. 'They're not going to do that, are they? Not when they've kept it a secret for so long. They're from a different generation, Flick, they're more private than us. Unless, of course . . .'

She breaks off and bites her lip.

'Unless, of course, what?'

'Unless Dad decides he wants to trace his real mother after all. Then they're going to have to talk about it.'

'Do you reckon he will?' My stomach does a somersault of excitement.

Ezzie thinks for a moment, then shakes her head emphatically. 'Nah. He was pretty clear on that score, wasn't he?'

I sigh in agreement. 'So, we'll never know. Perhaps it's just as well. I hate to think of Grandma and Grandpa upset.'

Ezzie laughs. 'Is that why you cheered them up with that daft game anyway. "*Just two kids and me and Ezzie?*" What are you like?'

'Made them laugh though!'

'Yeah, it did. But, come to think of it, that was strange too . . .'

'What?'

'Well . . . they've got two more, haven't they? But nobody mentioned them.'

'Two more what? Kids, d'you mean?' I say flippantly.

'No, idiot. Grandchildren.'

I'm so surprised, I come to a halt, my mouth hanging open.

'I forgot about them!' I'd actually forgotten that Grandma Liz and Grandpa Bert have got other grandchildren besides us. Aunty Libby's kids. Sam and Ellie. Aunty Libby and Uncle Jay's kids to be precise. They're my cousins!

But I've never met them.

Come to think of it, I'm not sure Grandma and Grandpa have met them either.

I wave out of the window to my fan club assembled on
the platform: Dad and Ezzie, and Amy who's run down
before school to wish me luck. Then I sling my overnight
bag in the luggage rack at the end of the carriage and
join Mum in our reserved seats. I keep my backpack with
me as it's full of things I want for the journey and pull
out a magazine. When I've flicked through it, eaten a bar
of chocolate, played some games on my phone and drunk
a can of Diet Coke, I take my book out and run my
hands over its velvety softness. My fingers trace the
delicate pattern of sequins, before opening it. I'm almost
reluctant to write on those pristine, pearly pages but I
promised Grandma I would, so I take a deep breath and
begin the saga of our journey, leaning on the table in
front of me. Ezzie's given me her best Parker ballpoint to
make sure there are no blotches, but it's quite hard
writing neatly with the train swaying from side to side.

Opposite me, Mum has lost interest in her paperback and is gazing out of the window, lost in her own world. She looks lovely today in slim black trousers and an ivory top, her suede jacket folded neatly on the seat beside her. She was at the hairdresser's at the crack of dawn, having her hair cut and blow-dried into a soft new urchin style that shows off her long neck.

I wish I could have a new style. There is absolutely nothing I can do with my hair, it has a mind of its own. If I cut it short, it curls up tight into a yellow, woolly skullcap and everyone thinks I'm a boy. If I try to grow it long, it reaches a certain length and digs its heels in, refusing to grow any more. It's too short to be scraped back; instead it hovers round my head like a giant puffball. Wherever I go, I am instantly recognizable. I know no one in the whole world with hair like mine except my father and at least his is dark and he can wear it cropped short.

My friends say they like it, it's cool, but it's all right for them. They don't have to go round looking as if they've just been nuked.

Which is why I've stuffed it under a beanie for now. Just for travelling, that is. It goes well with my favourite uniform: jeans, trainers and T-shirt. I've got my old check shirt on top too, because it was a bit chilly this morning.

'You *are* going to change for your audition, aren't

you?' Amy had squealed on the platform, eye~
and down. She's miffed with me because I've ~
down her this-season must-haves.

'Of course I am!' I say crossly. 'I've got my stuff
in my bag.'

I'm not sure about the clothes I'm wearing for the
audition. Mum had taken me out on Saturday and
bought me a whole new outfit: a new skirt, top, jacket,
tights and shoes. They're nice but they're all a bit
*matching*, if you know what I mean. I don't feel like me
in them. I like them individually, but with them all on
together I feel like a forty-year-old going to a wedding.

Anyway, I list them all carefully in my book so I
will remember what I wore in years to come, as
instructed by my grandmother, then I can't think of
anything else to write so I do an amusing little sketch of
my mother who has fallen asleep with her mouth open.
Then I read my magazine from cover to cover this time,
do a quiz to find out if I'm the type to nick my best
friend's boyfriend (no, I would not like to go out with
Mitch!), play a few more games and go over my article
for the audition. I can say it off by heart now. I consider
texting Amy but I haven't got much money on my
phone and I may need it for London.

Then I look out of the window.

I'm bored.

There's nothing to do.

Mum sleeps on, tired out from her early start, her face sagging deeper and deeper into her chest. Mmm, double chin. Not a good look. I do another quick sketch. She's not going to like it.

I wonder why young people look younger when
    they're asleep and old people look older?
I wonder where we are?
I wonder what time we're due into London?
I wonder when we're going to have lunch?
I wonder why I always get so hungry on trains?

I consider rousing my mother and asking her these questions but I figure she might not appreciate them, especially the first one, being as she's a bit testy when she first wakes up. I put my book away in my backpack, rooting through it for something to eat, but all I can find are some crisp crumbs which are soft and musty-tasting and one old chewing-gum minus its wrapping. I check my wallet and find Grandpa's twenty-pound note and another fiver nestling behind it. Yippee! I stuff the fiver in my back pocket and get to my feet, leaving my backpack on the table. I'm off to find food.

There's a huge queue at the buffet. A woman is interrogating the attendant about the ingredients of

every single ready-made sandwich on the s.
Behind her people clear their throats and raise them
eyebrows at each other.

In front of me, a tall boy with long, sun-streaked surfer
hair, wearing a blue Harley-Davidson T-shirt and baggy
jeans, shifts his weight from foot to foot, swaying lightly
with the movement of the train. He reminds me of a
skateboarder, or a snowboarder, or even someone riding
the waves. Suddenly the train slows down and he staggers
back on to *my* foot and I yelp. Immediately he turns, his
face alight with embarrassment. 'Sorry!' he says and his
hand shoots out to grab my arm and hold me steady. His
grip is strong. 'Are you OK?'

'Fine!' I say, then add before I can stop myself,
'Do you surf?'

'Yeah!' he says, his eyes lighting up to match his face.
'Do you?'

'No,' I say regretfully and it's my turn to feel an idiot,
but it's OK, he laughs.

'Pity,' he says and I make up my mind instantly that
I'm going to learn at the first possible opportunity.
He lets my arm go and smiles at me and I can't help
noticing how attractively his eyes crinkle up. But I can't
think of anything to say so I just grin back inanely
until he turns back to face the front. My face falls.
Amy, I need you here now, to help me with my flirting

technique! I wonder whether it's worth texting her.

But then, ahead of us, the woman finally makes her choice, tuna and cucumber on rye and a cup of decaffeinated tea, and the boy turns around again and whispers, 'Hurray!' under his breath and I smirk. Everyone shuffles forward. The next guy barks, 'Black coffee!' – no please or thank you whatsoever – and chucks his change on the counter for the attendant to pick up, like it's all his fault he's been kept waiting. The boy turns round and rolls his eyes at me and mouths a rude word about him and this time I giggle out loud. I don't mind waiting at all, but the queue's going down fast now.

Pity. I wish I could slow it down.

At last it's the boy's turn and he orders a coffee and then, unbelievably, he turns to me and says, 'Can I get you one?' and I'm so surprised I say, 'Yeah!' even though I never drink coffee normally; I was going to get myself a cold drink. *And* I forget to say please but he doesn't seem to mind, he just pays for the coffees and picks up the cardboard cups and says, 'Shall we sit down?' I follow him to a table and sit down opposite him. I can't believe my luck, but I'm scared stiff too because I don't know what to say.

But it turns out OK because he says, 'So you don't surf. What do you like doing then?' and I take a deep breath and decide to be honest. 'I like writing . . . and acting . . . and stuff like that,' and his face lights up again and he says, 'Me too! I was in my school's production of *Grease* last year!'

'And I was!'

We stare at each other in delight. 'I was Kenickie!' he says and I shriek, 'And I was Frenchy!' and the person on the next table looks up. We both laugh, because in the musical we're a couple and it occurs to me I should feel awkward, because the relationship was like, really serious, but I'm too curious.

'I can't imagine you as one of the T-Birds!' I laugh, remembering the gang of 1950s boys from Rydell High. He pulls out his wallet and says, 'Check it out!' in an American accent and hands me a photo. It's amazing, he looks completely different. His hair is shorter and dyed black and swept back into a quiff, and he's wearing a black leather jacket with the collar up and skin-tight jeans. He looks so much older.

'You look fantastic!' I say.

'Thanks. My dad helped me out. He's from the States. Bit of a Danny de Vito in his day! Have you got one of you as Frenchy?' I shake my head. He looks momentarily abashed. 'How sad do you think I am? I carry a photo around of me dressed as a T-Bird,' he says sheepishly.

I don't think he's sad at all. I think he's lovely. Especially now he's embarrassed.

'Drink your coffee,' he mumbles and I take a swig obediently, but I can't help pulling a face. 'What's up?' he asks and I say without thinking, 'I don't like coffee.' I could have bitten my tongue off.

'Why did you have one then?' he asks, puzzled.

I shrug. What have I got to lose. I'll probably never see him again. 'Because you asked me.'

'Cool,' he says and we beam at each other.

He is so easy to talk to. We've got loads in common. I don't have to think about the flirting technique I practised with Amy at all, we get on so well. He's nearly two years older than me, but he doesn't seem it. He's really funny as well. In fact, we're laughing and chatting so much we don't notice till the very last minute that the train has pulled into Paddington Station and everyone is getting off.

Not till my mother suddenly appears at my elbow from nowhere, that is. She's in a right tizz. Like I said, she's always grumpy when she wakes up. She's got her case in one hand and my backpack in the other and her jacket and handbag over her arm, and she completely ignores this really nice, cool boy and screeches at me in a most embarrassing and undignified fashion!

'So this is where you are! I've been up and down

this flaming train looking for you! Do you *want* to miss this audition?'

The next second she's yanked me up by the arm and hustled me off the train and into the crowd heading for the underground before I've had the chance to say 'Goodbye,' or 'Thanks for the coffee!' or 'Here's my number!' or anything. It is *so* humiliating!

But worse still, I suddenly realize that I don't even know the name of the one boy I've ever felt remotely interested in, and my heart plummets faster than the escalator which is whizzing me down into the bowels of the earth. I turn around and scan the crowds for him but this is real life, not a movie, and there's no one with blond-streaked, surfer-style hair and smiley grey-blue eyes, wearing a blue Harley-Davidson T-shirt and baggy jeans, climbing over their heads to get to me, like that Aussie guy in *Crocodile Dundee*, only better-looking.

And then, while I'm strap-hanging miserably in a crammed tube carriage on the way to the Television Centre, contemplating my broken heart and trying to use my backpack as a barrier between me and the armpit of the particularly large and sweaty man next to me, something suddenly occurs to me like a bolt out of the blue! Something that puts even my aborted relationship into perspective and drives all thoughts of thwarted love straight out of my head.

'Mum!' I whisper. She ignores me, sitting with her legs crossed, bags on her knees, still annoyed with me because of my disappearing act. 'Mum!' I say, more urgently this time. 'My bag!'

Her eyes fly to my backpack and she looks puzzled.

'My overnight bag! It's still on the train!'

It's sitting on the luggage rack at the end of Coach C to be precise. Where I left it. And in it are my clothes and my article for the audition.

'Felicity Pottery. She's here for an audition.'

My mother raps out my name to the receptionist and then turns to me and snaps, 'Don't slouch!'

She is in such a mood! She made us get off the tube and go all the way back to Paddington to fetch the case but when we got there, it was too late, the train had trundled off back the way it came carrying my bag with it.

'Doesn't anyone check if there's any luggage been left on the train!' fumes Mum when she finally finds someone official to talk to.

The man in uniform frowns. 'Nothing's been handed in, Madam. However, I'll try to contact the guard to see if it's still on the train, *when* I've got a minute.'

Mum opens her mouth to protest, thinks better of it and stands meekly to one side while he deals with a million other enquiries. Finally, he disappears for what seems like hours, and Mum starts cursing under her breath and sending me death looks again. At last he returns.

'Good news!' he says, smiling. 'It's been found.'

'Thank goodness for that!' Mum sighs in relief. 'Where is it?'

'On its way to Exeter!' says the man. 'I've arranged for it to be placed in the guard's van, under lock and key.'

'Exeter!' wails Mum. 'We need it here! Now!'

The man's smile vanishes. 'I'm afraid that's impossible, Madam. Now if you don't mind, I'm rather busy . . .'

He takes himself away into his office, visibly affronted at her obvious lack of appreciation of all his hard work. Mum stamps her foot and turns into a Rottweiler, baring her teeth at me.

'This is all your fault!' she snarls, looking as if she'd like to tear my throat out. 'We're going to be late now!'

I would like to point out that, strictly speaking, it's actually her fault, because she was the person who hustled me off the train before I had time to remember my bag, but I think maybe this would not be a good idea.

She chivvies me out of the station, snapping at my heels to make sure I keep up with her, and bundles me into a taxi. I feel a moment's pleasure as I sink on to the back seat: I've always wanted to go in a black London cab. But then it starts wending its way very, very slowly indeed through the manic stream of traffic and Mum's eyes start alternating between her watch and the meter that is, ironically, clocking up the fare like a speed dial on a formula one racing car, and I start to feel sick.

By the time we get to the Television Centre and Mum has handed over a week's housekeeping to the cab driver, she's having a nervous breakdown and I just want to go home.

The girl on the reception desk takes down our particulars and speaks into the phone. 'Someone will be with you in a minute,' she announces, sounding bored out of her skull. 'Take a seat.' Ten minutes later we're still sitting there and Mum's fretting her head off.

'It's all your fault,' she repeats for the umpteenth time as if I hadn't already worked that one out, and I shrink into my seat, trying to make myself invisible as she rants away to herself, like a mad woman.

'I don't know what your father's going to say,' she mutters, then, 'I'm sure that taxi driver robbed us!'

She continues chuntering away in like fashion under her breath while the minutes tick by. The receptionist looks at her once or twice in alarm then comes to the conclusion she's harmless and starts filing her nails. People begin to drift out of the building on their way to lunch and the hands of the clock keep turning. Mum gets to her feet, folds her arms in front of her, always a bad sign, and starts pacing up and down the reception area.

'I'm sure they've forgotten all about us,' she says, glaring at the girl on the desk as if she holds her personally responsible. The girl, oblivious to Mum's death looks, carries on with her manicure.

Then the lift opposite us opens and two people step out: a tall guy with grey hair, wearing jeans and jacket with a T-shirt underneath, and a young woman with masses of auburn hair tumbling round her shoulders, dressed in black leggings and a long pink and black stripy top. She's carrying a big purple bag and has a number of brightly-coloured scarves wound round her neck. She looks cool. They're deep in conversation.

'The girl with the long hair was very confident . . .' I hear the man say.

'So was the boy,' answers the young woman.

'They all were,' agrees the man. 'Hard to choose between them . . .' They make for the exit, continuing their conversation, the man holding the door open before him for the woman to pass through.

'Mr Cambriani!' calls the receptionist, glancing up from her nails just as they're about to disappear. 'Felicity Pottery here to see you.'

The couple come to a halt and look at each other. 'Good grief,' says the man, retracing his steps. 'We'd given up on you!' He smiles at me pleasantly and shakes

Mum by the hand. 'I'm Greg Cambriani and this is my assistant, Tabitha.'

'I'm sorry we're so late,' says Mum, grabbing his hand like a lifeline. 'We've had a terrible time getting here.'

Mr Cambriani pats her hand. 'I'm sorry, Mrs Pottery,' he says, trying to disentangle himself, 'but I'm afraid Felicity has missed the auditions. We have a very busy schedule, you know.'

'Please!' Mum says in alarm. 'She's been so looking forward to this! We've come all this way!'

Mr Cambriani shakes his head regretfully. 'I'm very sorry. We've run out of studio time.' Tabitha smiles at me ruefully.

My heart sinks. Next to me I can feel Mum oozing disappointment like a deflated balloon.

The lift door opens again and six people get out this time, chatting excitedly. I realize who they are straight away. There's a tall girl with long hair and a fringe, real head girl material, with a posh man who I assume is her dad; behind her is another exceptionally pretty, very glamorous girl, with her mum, presumably, though she could possibly be her older sister; and then there's a boy, his hair gelled into artful spikes, with his mother in tow. All of them are dressed from top to toe in this-season, high-street chic and look incredibly self-assured. It's pretty obvious they've been for the audition.

It's also pretty obvious none of them notice me at all. Instead, their faces break into radiant smiles when they spot Mr Cambriani and Tabitha, and Spiky-Haired Boy high-fives them with much shrieking of jolly laughter from the whole company, though I can't help noticing Glamour-Girl's mum (definitely her mum, I've spotted the crow's feet now I'm up close) and Posh Dad seem just a little put out by this overdose of familiarity.

They chat and smile and shriek a lot and then, eventually, they all make a noisy exit, with lots of handshakes from Posh and her dad and hugs from Glamour-Girl and her mum and more high fives from Spiky-Hair, but not from his mum, thank goodness.

It's *blatantly obvious* that they've all had the most amazing auditions and are now best mates with Mr Cambriani.

I hate gelled spikes.

And posh head girls.

And exceptionally pretty, glamorous girls who are clones of their mums.

I sigh heavily.

Mr Cambriani looks down at me as if he's forgotten my existence.

'My dad's going to go bananas when he knows I've missed the audition,' I say conversationally. 'It's all my fault, you see.'

110

Mr Cambriani looks uncomfortable.

'I left my bag on the train.'

'That's tough,' he says sympathetically.

'It had all my new clothes in it we bought for the audition.'

'That's really tough!' says Tabitha.

I shrug. 'I didn't like them anyway. They weren't me. But they cost a lot. So did the train fare. And the taxi across London because we were late. And my mum had to take time off work. This whole trip has been pretty expensive actually.'

Mum looks as if she's about to cry.

Mr Cambriani looks strained. 'I wish there was something I could do . . .' he murmurs. 'But the studio is already booked out this afternoon.'

Tabitha coughs. 'We could nip in now!' she says, from the side of her mouth, like I'm not meant to hear.

'What about lunch?' Mr Cambriani mouths back, like I'm not meant to see.

'I can be really quick!' I say and pull my beanie off my head in excitement. My hair springs up to attention around my head and everyone, even Mum, laughs.

'Great hair!' says Tabitha admiringly. I really like Tabitha.

'OK,' says Mr Cambriani, suddenly, decisively. 'We'll see if we can squeeze you in! But we'll have to be quick. Follow me.'

Mum and Tabitha beam with pleasure.

Suddenly, having got what I want, I hold back.

'What is it?' asks Tabitha.

'Like this?' I ask, looking down dubiously at my worn jeans, my T-shirt and my old check shirt.

Mr Cambriani appraises me carefully, then he does what everyone else does.

He ruffles my hair.

'I think you look perfect,' he says. His eyes crinkle at the corners when he smiles.

I really like Mr Cambriani too.

The audition is fun. There's no time to be nervous. We go up to the studio and Tabitha runs around persuading cameramen and technicians and people to work through their lunch-break and everyone groans but nobody seems to mind that much.

I have to read my piece to camera.

'Where's your article?' asks Mum, starting to fuss.

'In my overnight bag,' I say and her face drops. So does Mr Cambriani's and Tabitha's. 'It's OK, 'I say hastily, 'I know it off by heart, anyway.'

'Good girl,' says Mr Cambriani and we begin. Tabitha gives me the thumbs up, just as the camera starts to roll and I give her a big grin in return. She's hovering behind the shoulder of the cameraman, and I decide to say my piece straight to her, like I would to Amy, because she's starting to feel like a mate. At the end, Mr Cambriani winks at me. We must have had less time than he thought because after I'd done it once, he said that was enough, even though he'd said it would take two or three takes.

Then he asks me to read another piece to camera. It's a transcript of the commentary on last year's Wimbledon Men's Final. I'd watched it on telly because I'd been home with a sore throat so it's easy-peasy. And I remember the American should have challenged a point because the ball was out but he didn't and that's when his luck turned against him, so I put that bit in to make it more interesting. Mr Cambriani turns to Tabitha and raises his eyebrows then and I think, 'Trust me!' and wish I'd stuck to the script.

Afterwards he says, 'That's fine, Felicity,' and I say, 'Flick. My name's Flick,' and he crosses my name out and writes it down again on the form. Then he says, 'Now then, Flick, is there anything else you want to say to camera while you've got the chance,' and I say, 'What do you mean? Like, do you want me to sing a song or something?' hoping he will say no, but he smiles and says, 'If you like. You've got a few minutes to fill. I want to see what you can do.'

What can I do? Nothing. I can't sing (OK, I know I had a role in *Grease* but it was Frenchy and in our version she was the Pink Lady with the terrible voice), I don't know any jokes except rude ones and I can't remember a single line of poetry. I can feel everyone staring at me but my mind has gone blank. I've got to do something. I take a deep breath. There's one thing I'm always good at. Daddy or chips.

'Would you rather . . . ?'

There's a long pause while I sift desperately through my head to pluck an interesting philosophical choice from the mush my brain has turned into.

Everyone waits politely.

Tabitha nods at me encouragingly. Inspiration! I open my mouth and it comes out in a rush.

'Would you rather take Tabitha out to lunch or audition me?'

There's a stunned silence followed by roars of laughter, whistles and cheers from everyone in the studio except for Mr Cambriani who looks surprised, Tabitha who looks a bit pink and Mum who covers her eyes and groans.

'It's a serious question,' I frown at the technical crew. 'You don't have to decide in a rush,' I explain to Mr Cambriani. 'And you can ask questions.'

He stares at me, nonplussed. Luckily Tabitha gets it. 'I've played something like this in the pub! Does he have to pay for lunch?'

'Of course.'

Mr Cambriani grins. The penny's dropped. 'Do I get to choose the restaurant?'

'No. Tabitha does.'

Tabitha gives a cheer. Mr Cambriani looks disappointed. 'Pity, she's vegetarian.'

'Does Greg have to come straight back to work afterwards?' leers the soundman with the microphone. The rest of the room laughs.

'Absolutely,' I say sternly, knowing exactly what he's getting at, and he looks a bit shamefaced. Then they all start firing questions at me, though I notice most of them are to do with Mr Cambriani and Tabitha and less are about me and the actual audition, and I have to keep my wits about me, fielding them all.

In fact, I'm beginning to think everyone in the room, including Mr Cambriani, has forgotten the real reason we are actually here because they all seem to be having such a good time playing Daddy or chips, when a smartly dressed woman, all high heels, fitted jacket, specs and hair piled up on top of her head, walks in and says in surprise, 'What's going on in here? I thought this studio was booked out to us this afternoon?'

'It is! We just borrowed it for a bit but we're done now,' says Mr Cambriani. The woman nods and walks back out again. 'Thanks very much, Flick,' he adds. 'I think we all enjoyed that!'

'But you must decide!' I insist. 'Audition me or take Tabitha to lunch?' The room falls silent.

'Audition you! Definitely!'

A cheer goes up around the room and I get a round of applause from everyone, including the pervy soundman.

'That was great!' laughs Tabitha. She leans over and whispers theatrically in my ear. 'I'd rather listen to you than go to lunch with Greg any day!'

'Shame,' he says. 'Because I was going to suggest we tried that new vegan place round the corner!' Tabitha pulls a sorry face but he says, 'Too late!' and bends down to shake my hand. 'Thanks for that, Flick. I'll be in touch.'

Suddenly I feel flat. Is that it?

'When?'

'Soon.' His face, close to mine, is serious, then he winks at me and repeats, 'Soon. I promise.'

Mum and I go to check in at our hotel. It's just around the corner from the television studios so we can walk to it. 'Thank goodness,' says Mum. 'I don't think I've got a lot left in my purse. I'd better get some money out for dinner tonight.'

But when we check in, we have a nice surprise. The TV studios have booked us in for dinner, bed and breakfast, so it's all paid for! And our room is fantastic!

It's got its own private bathroom with a basin that sort

of balances on top of a marble unit, and a shower as well. It's all white and shiny and chrome and new, with stacks of shampoo and shower gels and creams and soaps that Mum says are complimentary, which means we can help ourselves and take them home if we want to.

The bedroom is beautiful, with everything matching – curtains, bedspreads, the lot – and twin beds, piled up high with sumptuous pillows and cushions.

'Bags me the one by the window!' I shout and dive on to the bed, wallowing in its silky softness. There's a brown leather sofa to sit on too and a low coffee table with loads of magazines. There's tea and coffee and drinking chocolate you can help yourself to and different kinds of biscuits. Mum makes us a cup of tea straight away and we attack the chocolate chips because we haven't had any lunch and we're starving.

But best of all there's a huge television that has every single channel under the sun, including foreign ones, and you can rent out DVDs if you want to.

'This is brilliant!' I say, surfing through the channels. 'It's got Sky Plus as well. Are all hotels like this?'

'I don't think so,' says Mum, opening cupboard doors and peering inside. 'Not that I'm a connoisseur. Look, there's a hairdryer in here. And a trouser press! Ooh, I wish I'd known. I could have brought all your dad's trousers with me and given them a good going over.'

I hope she's not serious. 'What's this?' I ask, opening a small cupboard door. Inside is a fridge, stacked full of wine, cans, chocolate and crisps. 'Wow, Mum, look at all this! Is this complimentary as well?'

'I don't know,' says Mum. She consults a list on the inside of the door. 'Oh my goodness, Flick, close it up quick! I'm not paying that for a Kit Kat!'

I slam the door shut before it costs us money.

'What shall we do?' I ask. 'It's ages till dinnertime.'

Mum eyes me critically. 'I think we should go and get you something decent to wear,' she says. 'You can't go to dinner dressed like that.'

'We're going to go shopping!' I say, surprised. 'Can we afford it?'

'No,' says Mum, stuffing her purse in her bag. 'But it's not every day we stay at a posh hotel like this for free and that's all down to you. So come on, wild child, let's hit town!'

I jump off the bed, delighted. I love it when Mum throws caution to the wind and lets her hair down, like she did that time she tried to book the holiday. I even forgive her the dodgy teen-speak!

We go to Oxford Street because Mum says it's good for shopping and we have a fabulous time. We dip in and out of shops and try on loads of stuff, both of us, most of which we have no intention of buying. Mum tries on this black ruffled silk dress and I know where the phrase 'looking a million dollars' comes from now, because she looks sensational in it. When she checks the price, it's not quite that much but it is, actually, over a thousand quid! She doesn't turn a hair! Like, I'd be scared stiff I'd put my foot through it or something but she just giggles and picks up this designer handbag and says, 'Do you think this would go with it?' and, I kid you not, it cost nearly eight hundred pounds! For a bag! When she comes out of the changing room she hands the dress back to the assistant regretfully. 'It's not quite what I was looking for, thank you,' she says, and the woman looks disappointed, like she was expecting Mum to buy it.

I never knew my Mum could be that cool.

But then she buys herself a cardi from M&S and I think, she's not that cool after all.

Me, I get a pair of jeans and a stripy top to wear tonight, like the one Tabitha was wearing. I expect Mum to say it's not smart enough for the hotel but I think Tabitha's opened her eyes a bit and showed her that smart doesn't have to mean formal. She says *if* we ever catch up with my overnight bag, we can take the other clothes back because she's still got the receipt and, let's face it, I'm never going to wear them anywhere else, am I? Which I could have told her in the first place.

Then I blow the twenty pounds Grandpa gave

me on a selection of brightly-coloured scarves, just like Tabitha's.

When we get back to the hotel having stuffed ourselves on cappuccinos, milk shakes and chocolate fudge bakes at a trendy little café ('Don't tell your father how much we paid for a cup of coffee and a bit of cake, will you?' gasps Mum when she sees the bill), we have a surprise. Tabitha and Greg Cambriani are sitting in the foyer, waiting for us. They get to their feet, smiling.

'I've bought a top like yours,' I say shyly, opening the bag to show Tabitha. 'And some scarves.'

'Brilliant,' she says, putting her arm around my shoulders and giving me a squeeze. 'You'll be able to wear them when you do your report.'

'What report?' I ask.

I WON!!!!!!!!!!!!!

I still can't believe it! I won the competition!

Mr Cambriani . . . Greg, I mean, that's what he said I must call him . . . Greg said he and Tabitha came to their decision over lunch and so they thought they might as well come and tell me now.

'It wasn't difficult,' says Greg. 'I knew you were the one as soon as you started talking.'

'No, before that,' says Tabitha. 'As soon as you smiled at the camera. Brilliant!'

'Your piece on Wimbledon was great too,' chips in Greg. 'You showed a bit of initiative there.'

'Phew! I thought I'd blown it,' I admit.

'Not at all. And that choice you gave me . . .' Greg chuckles, 'well, I think everyone enjoyed that. Especially the way you handled all the questions.'

'Sheer genius!' agrees Tabitha. I smile modestly,

basking in their praise.

'You're a natural,' says Greg. 'Have you done much of this before?'

'She's got an aunt in television,' says Mum, proud as punch. 'Maybe it runs in the blood.'

'Have you?' asks Tabitha. 'What's her name?'

'Libby,' I answer. 'Libby Ryder.'

There's silence. Tabitha and Greg stare at me in disbelief.

'You're kidding!' says Greg.

'No, it's true,' says Mum. 'She's my husband's sister. Though, actually, I've never met her.'

'You have you know,' interrupts Tabitha excitedly. 'You met her this morning!'

'Where?' I ask blankly.

'At the studio.'

I rack my brains in surprise. Oh no, it must be misery-guts on the front desk, the one obsessed with her nails. How disappointing. Typical family story this, that gets bigger in the telling. Famous Aunty Libby who works in television is just a receptionist.

Greg shakes his head like it's a really big deal. 'Well, well, well. I've worked with Libby many times. She's one of the best in the business. So enthusiastic about her job.'

There you are then. Just shows how wrong you

can be. To me she looked as if she was bored out of her skull.

'Which one was she then?' asks Mum, who's obviously as surprised as I am.

'You remember the woman who came in to ask if the studio was free?' says Tabitha. 'That's Libby Ryder. She's really successful you know. Everyone wants to work with Libby.'

A smart woman, hair up, businesslike. I remember. That was my aunty! And I didn't even know.

'Would you like me to give her a ring?' asks Greg, taking his mobile out of his pocket. 'I'm sure she'd love to meet with you.'

'I don't know . . .' says Mum, looking unconvinced. 'We're only here for the one night . . .'

'All the more reason for you to get together,' says Greg firmly. 'Libby's great, you'll love her.'

Mum doesn't look persuaded. She'd been looking forward to us dressing up and going down to dinner together.

'Go on, Mum,' I say, shaking her arm. 'Grandma would be so pleased if we met up with her!'

'All right then,' she says reluctantly. 'Though I expect she'll be too busy at this late notice.'

Greg presses the speed dial on his phone.

★ ★ ★

124

She wasn't too busy. Or if she was, she managed to rearrange things. She'd join us for dinner, she said, if that was all right with us.

'Of course!' says Mum into Greg's mobile. 'That would be lovely.' But I'm not sure she means it because she looks a bit strained and she's putting her posh voice on.

Greg and Tabitha run through a few details with us about what will happen next. They're going to arrange for me to report on a big sports event for a special children's news programme they're putting together.

'Is there anything particular you would like to cover?' asks Tabitha but I shake my head.

'I like all kinds of sport,' I say. 'I don't mind at all.'

'We'll run through the fixtures that are on over the next few weeks and get back to you asap,' says Greg. 'I'll need the name of your head teacher to get permission in case we have to take you out of school in term-time. We're looking Europe-wide so you may have to miss school for a few days.'

'Shame!' I say and Greg grins.

'The sacrifices we have to make, eh? Got a passport?'

'I've applied for one.' Mum and I exchange a wry smile.

'Must have known you were going to need it! Well, I think that should do for now. We'll be in touch, Mrs Pottery.'

'Jo.'

'Jo, it is.' He shakes her hand. 'Great to meet you, Flick.'

'Get back to you soon,' says Tabitha, planting a kiss on my cheek. 'Now go and get your glad rags on and have a lovely dinner.'

'They are so nice,' says Mum as we wave goodbye to them, then she squeals and envelops me in her arms. 'You clever, clever girl! I'm so proud of you! You're going to be on the telly!'

'All worth it then, in the end?' I grin, my face squashed uncomfortably into her neck.

'You bet!' she says. 'Let's tell your dad and Ez.' She grabs her phone from her bag and presses 'home', her face alight with excitement, but it goes to answerphone. 'Blast!' she says. 'I'm not leaving a message, I want to surprise them. I'll wait till later. Right then,' she grins at me in delight. 'Now for dinner! Bags me the first shower!'

'Race you for it!' I say and dart ahead, squeezing into a lift just as the doors are closing. The last thing I see is Mum madly pressing buttons to call down another lift. When I turn around, grinning my head off, I'm confronted by an elevator full of disapproving faces. I cough and study my feet intently, but I still can't wipe that smile off my face, no matter how hard I try.

By the time we're ready for dinner we've emptied every complimentary on the bathroom shelf and price tags from our new clothes are scattered all over the floor. I feel great. My new jeans feel like I've been poured into them, and I love my stripy top. I pick up my blue book and a pen. You never know, I might want to make a note of things in the restaurant. I'm a writer now!

But Mum's feeling edgy. She's wearing a lovely new mustard yellow dress which she'd bought especially for the trip to London. It makes her look really slim but curvy at the same time, but she's not happy, I can tell. She keeps doing that thing where she stands sideways to the mirror and smoothes her hands over her stomach. Then she starts changing her shoes and muttering under her breath, always a tell-tale sign.

'What's wrong?' I ask.

'I'm not sure about this dress,' she moans.

'You look fantastic.'

'It's the colour . . .' she says, hopping about on one foot. She gets her shoe on and glares at herself in the mirror. 'And the shape . . .' She musses up her hair, like that would make a difference to the dress, and pouts at her reflection. 'Do you think it's too short?'

'No,' I say, genuinely surprised. 'Anyway, what does it matter? You're only going for something to eat.

You'll be sitting down most of the time. No one will see you.'

She darts me a look of venom. 'I've still got to walk in, haven't I? I don't want to look tarty.'

'You don't look tarty!' I say, bemused. I nearly add, 'You couldn't look tarty if you tried,' because, let's face it, she's not far off forty and that's a bit past tartiness if you ask me, but something tells me she might still want to be able to look tarty if she felt like it.

'I bet she doesn't really want to meet us anyway,' she mutters.

'Who?' I ask, puzzled.

'Your amazing Aunty Libby,' she says tartly.

So that's what this is about! 'Of course she does!'

'Hmm. She didn't seem too keen on the phone to me. She started to make excuses. But someone in the background was telling her to go. It must have been Jay, her husband.'

'Well that's all right then.' Mum doesn't look convinced. So I say, 'You look sensational, Mum, honest. I hope I look like you when I'm . . .' I nearly say 'old' but with amazing quick thinking, I tactfully substitute the words 'your age'.

It works. She fluffs up her hair, sprays herself with a generous dollop of perfume and picks up her bag.

'Thank you, darling,' she says and grabs me by

the hand. 'Come on, Felicity Pottery. Let's show Libby Flaming Ryder we're not all yokels where we come from.'

Mum is so funny. She's freaking out in the bedroom because she's not sure if she looks OK, but as soon as we step out of the lift into the foyer it's like she's had a confidence transplant. She swans into the restaurant as if she does this every night of the week and gives our room number to the guy on the desk who's all dressed up in a dinner jacket and bow tie.

It's dead swanky inside, with round tables covered in white linen tablecloths that reach all the way down to the floor and high-backed chairs with upholstered seats. A waiter escorts us to our table next to a tall window draped in thick swathes of curtains, the same deep blue as the carpet. In the middle of the table is a single white flower in a dainty vase and there are four place-settings, each with a confusing amount of cutlery, two wine glasses of different sizes and a blue napkin folded into a concertina. The waiter pulls our chairs out for us to sit down. No one's ever done that for me before.

'Will anyone be joining you for dinner, Madam?' he asks, offering us menus with a flourish.

'Just one guest,' says Mum without hesitating, as if she's asked that question all the time. She's using her posh voice again. She orders a glass of dry white wine for herself and fresh orange juice for me while we decide what we want to eat. When it comes, my juice really is fresh; it's got bits of real orange floating about in it. I sip it, studying the menu in complete bewilderment.

'What's sashimi?'

'Haven't a clue,' says Mum.

'What's prosciutto?'

'I'm not sure. It's Italian. It might be bread. Like bruschetta, or whatever it's called.'

'Five pounds ninety-five for bread!'

'Maybe it's ham? Anyway, don't worry, we're not paying! Choose something else if you don't like the sound of it.'

'Monkfish cheeks!' This is getting worse. I didn't even know monkfish had cheeks. 'I don't think there's anything I can eat on this menu.'

'Don't be silly. There are lots of lovely things here.' Mum scans down the menu. 'What about moules mariniere?'

'What's that?'

'Mussels.'

'No way!'

'OK then, carpaccio of venison and pickled figs with . . .'

'Venison?' My jaw falls open in horror. 'Isn't that . . . ?'

'Deer. Yes you're right. How about the veal?'

'Veal?'

'Baby calf. Perhaps not.' Mum's starting to look a bit fraught. 'What about saffron-infused cod brandade with pan-fried purple potatoes? You'd like that.'

'I don't even know what it is!'

'Fish and chips,' says a voice at my elbow. 'You must be Jo and Flick. Mind if we join you?'

I look up startled. A woman is smiling down at me. She's got shoulder-length brown hair with gold highlights and glasses perched on top of her head. She's wearing plain trousers and a dark, silky shirt and hardly any make-up. Beside her is a girl, some years younger than me, dressed in jeans and T-shirt.

'I'm Libby and this is my daughter Ellie,' the woman explains. 'I hope it's OK to bring her with me. Jay is working tonight and Sam's out and I couldn't leave her on her own,'

Mum and I scramble to our feet. 'You don't look a bit like you did earlier on!' I say in surprise.

Libby laughs. 'Power dressing! I find it helps at work. I

turn back into me once I get home. A bit of a scruff-bag.'

She doesn't look a scruff-bag. She looks casual but stylish, as if her clothes cost a lot of money even if they are just for lounging about in. I think Mum feels the same because I can see her eyeing them.

'I recognized you straight away,' says Libby, 'even from the back.'

'How come?' I'm puzzled. 'I didn't think you noticed me in the studio.'

'I didn't. Sorry about that. I was too intent on getting my studio back.' She looks a bit ashamed of herself. 'It's your hair,' she continues. 'It's just like Martin's. Different colour, but the way it stands out around your head, Martin's does that.'

Mum snorts. 'That shows how long it is since you last saw him then. He hasn't worn it like that since before we got married. You didn't make it to the wedding, did you?'

I glance at Mum, surprised at her tone. She sounds a bit rude. Libby must think so too because pink flares into her cheeks and she says, 'No, I'm afraid I didn't. I was working in the States at the time,' and she has a really sorry expression on her face. Mum looks abashed.

'He wears it cropped short now,' she explains, more gently this time. 'Has done for years.'

'I think your hair is lovely.' Ellie is smiling shyly up at

133

me. She reminds me of someone when she smiles but I can't think who.

'Thanks. I like yours too.' It's fine and straight and shaped into a neat, well-behaved bob, the complete opposite of my wild frizz. 'And I like your alphabet necklace.' Her name is suspended around her neck like an identity badge in bright, sparkly letters.

'I had it for my birthday from my brother Sam.'

'Cool brother.'

She nods happily. She's at that cute, skinny, straight-up-and-down stage and she has bright curious eyes that peep inquisitively through her fringe. 'He's *in luurve*,' she drawls.

'Since when?' asks her mum in alarm.

'Since today,' she says and we all laugh.

'News to me,' Libby says. 'It's hard to keep track of him nowadays.'

Mum gives her a sympathetic look. 'Mothers are always the last to know. Shall we sit down?'

Libby takes the seat next to me. Her eyes fall on my blue book and she stiffens.

'Where did you get that?' she asks.

'Grandma gave it to me when I won this audition. It belonged to her. Her father bought it for her as a prize for getting into university but she couldn't go because he died.'

'I know.' She pauses then adds, 'She offered it to me when I went.'

'Why didn't you accept it?' I say, puzzled. 'It's beautiful.'

'It is,' she agrees. 'I don't know. I didn't really want to go. I suppose it felt more like a bribe than a reward.' She gives a wry little laugh. 'I was very mixed up at the time.'

I can't imagine sophisticated Libby Ryder being a mixed-up teenager.

I think Mum felt bad about being a bit shirty to her because soon she's back to her normal friendly self and before long they're both chatting away, nineteen to the dozen. Dinner turns out to be surprisingly edible after all and they wash it down with a bottle of the best French sav blanc from the wine list that Libby says is definitely worth the extra.

'Anyway, it's my treat,' she says, but Mum says, 'No! This is all on the television studios!' and then she laughs and says wonderingly, 'Listen to me, I can't believe this is all happening!' Libby looks around the table at her and Ellie and me and her eyes go all soft and crinkly again and she says, 'Neither can I, isn't it lovely?' But I think she means meeting us because suddenly she puts her arm around my shoulders and squeezes me tight.

She's nice, my Aunty Libby.

'Do I call you Aunty?' I ask, looking up at her.

She thinks for a minute, considering. 'It's probably a bit late for that,' she says regretfully. 'Just call me Libby.'

'Well you can definitely call me Aunty Jo,' says Mum emphatically to Ellie. 'I'm been dying for someone to call me Aunty all my life.'

'OK then,' says Ellie obligingly. 'But Sam won't. He'll just call you Jo.'

'Sam will be seventeen this year,' explains Libby.

'Practically grown up,' says Mum.

'He thinks he is,' says Libby. 'You think you know it all at that age, don't you?' She sighs heavily and rests her chin on her hands.

She looks sad. I wonder if Sam is a bad boy who gives her grief? Maybe he's out right now, dealing drugs or stealing cars.

Mum must be wondering the same thing because she's silent for a moment then she gives a little cough and says, 'Our Ezzie is seventeen.'

'Yes, she must be,' says Libby. She's lost in her own world, her thoughts elsewhere, with Bad Boy Sam I should think.

'Actually, Ezzie's finding life a bit hard at the moment,' says Mum confidingly.

'Is she?' Libby's tone is polite but her eyes are still downcast.

'She's pregnant.'

'No! Really?' Libby's eyes open wide with shock.

'I'm afraid so.'

Libby moistens her lips with the tip of her tongue. 'Is she going to keep it?'

Mum nods. 'She's pretty far gone now.'

'She wouldn't have had an abortion, if that's what you mean,' I say fiercely. 'Ezzie wouldn't do that.'

'I didn't mean that,' says Libby hastily. 'I just wondered . . . Isn't she off to university? Medicine, isn't it?'

'Well, all her plans are on hold at the minute,' says Mum, glancing at her curiously. 'How did you know that?'

'Mum keeps me informed. She writes me a long letter every so often telling me what you've all been up to.'

Mum looks surprised. 'But she didn't tell you her granddaughter was pregnant?'

'No, she didn't tell me that.' Libby bites her lip. 'Poor Ezzie.'

Mum shakes her head impatiently. 'It's not the end of the world! Though your mother thinks it is. She's taken it really badly. She's from that generation who thought a baby born out of wedlock was something to be ashamed of.'

'She wants Ezzie to have the baby adopted,' I explain.

Libby grimaces. 'Now why doesn't that surprise me?

Brush it all under the carpet, that's Mum. Pretend it never happened.' She looks as if she's going to cry. 'Is there a father around?'

Mum makes a funny little noise in her throat, a mixture of a chuckle and a sob. 'His name's Spud. Ezzie collects waifs and strays. He's one of them. Martin's not best pleased, I can tell you.'

'Dad thinks Spud's all right now, Mum. Since we had the party the other night.'

'That was just the beer talking,' says Mum shortly. 'Anyway, it doesn't matter what your dad thinks of him at the end of the day. It's what Ezzie thinks that matters.'

There's a silence, like we're all lost in our own thoughts, except for Ellie who's getting bored with the conversation and starting to yawn. Libby notices and says gently, 'Time to make tracks?' and Ellie nods.

'I'm full as a gug,' she says sleepily. I stare at her in surprise.

'That's what we say! What is a gug?'

Libby laughs. 'I've no idea! I've always said it.'

'Dad does too. We all do, it's a family thing!' I say and we smile at each other with satisfaction. I like Libby.

She gathers their stuff together and fishes round in her handbag for a card for Mum. 'These are my details,' she says. 'You must come and stay with us next time you're in London. We've got plenty of room.'

'Thank you,' says Mum. 'We'd like that. I might even be able to persuade Martin to come, you never know. He never wants to go anywhere.'

Libby looks wistful. 'It would be good to see him again after all these years.'

The two women smile at each other then suddenly Libby leans forward and gives Mum a hug. 'Don't listen to my mother,' she says. 'Let Ezzie make her own mind up what she wants to do. Otherwise she'll spend her whole life regretting it.'

'We will, don't you worry,' says Mum, patting Libby on the back. Weirdly, it looks like she's comforting Libby, not the other way round. 'We'll support her every step of the way.' She sighs heavily. 'Whatever she decides.'

It's not till we get back to our hotel bedroom that night and I pick up my phone and see the millions of messages from Amy and Ezzie that I realize we'd forgotten to tell them I'd won! Mum had said we had to leave our phones in the bedroom when we went down for dinner, because it was bad manners to have them going off in the dining room (even though everyone else's did!), and then we'd got so excited by Libby and Ellie turning up like that we'd completely forgotten to let them know! Mum says I'm allowed one quick phone call to each of them because it's so late. I call Ezzie and Dad first on Mum's mobile.

'YAY!!!!!!!!!!!!!!!!!!!!!!!!' screeches Ezzie down the phone when she hears the news.

'Did she win?' I hear Dad in the background. 'Did she win?' He must have grabbed the phone off her because he bellows in my ear, 'DID YOU WIN?' like his brain's turned into chewing-gum and has stuck fast to that particular question.

'Yes, Dad, I did.'

I hold the phone at arm's length as my father's voice leaps into our hotel bedroom in a raucous, braying whoop of triumph. Mum and I laugh.

'I knew you would! I said you'd win, didn't I? That's my girl.' He makes it sound as if it's all due to him and the faith he had in me. Actually, if I remember rightly, it was Grandma who said I'd win, plus Amy, of course. I seem to recall Mum and him arguing over who was going to take me to London because neither of them thought I'd get past the first round.

'It's just an audition, Dad, not the Olympic Games!' I say modestly but secretly I'm chuffed by his reaction. Then he asks, 'Where are we off to then? Is it the Champions League Final?' and I say indignantly, 'Is that all you care about?'

'No, no, of course not!' he splutters and I go, 'Yeah, right!' but I have to laugh, because he's so obvious.

'Tell him he's going to have to apply for that passport, after all,' says Mum. 'Looks as if he might need it.'

'Tell him yourself,' I say and hand the phone to her but instead she says, 'Hey, Martin? Never guess who we've been with tonight.' She pauses while Dad obviously makes some wildly amusing guesses because she screeches like a banshee and then says, 'I wish! No, it was your sister. Yes, Libby, that's right! And Ellie, her daughter.'

Mum and Dad carry on yacking away and I decide to ring Amy on my phone while they're at it. She reacts predictably, shrieking her head off, and makes me go step by step through the audition in minute detail.

'I can't believe you had to wear your old clothes!' she shrieks, then when she hears I played Daddy or chips she nearly has hysterics. To change the subject I ask her what she's been up to since she waved me off on the train this morning, which seems a lifetime ago.

Daft question. I'm treated to a day in the life of Mitch, super-stud. Apparently Mitch got into trouble at school today for being rude to a teacher *(nothing new there then!)* but people have got him wrong *(says Amy!)* because he's not arrogant *(not half!)* he's just confident *(big-headed!)* and people can't handle that, especially teachers *(especially me!)*, and if they only took the trouble to get to know him properly they would see that . . .

My brain switches off from the Mitch Admiration Society and wanders away to another boy instead.

A tall boy with sun-streaked hair and smiley grey-blue eyes, wearing a Harley-Davidson T-shirt.
A boy who bought me a disgusting cup of coffee and made me laugh.

A boy without a shred of arrogance but brave enough to dye his hair black, slick it into a quiff, turn up the collar of his black leather jacket and perform songs from *Grease* in front of the whole school.

A boy who carries a photo of himself round with him dressed as a T-Bird.

A boy so easy to talk to I didn't notice we'd pulled into Paddington Station until my mother came and dragged me away from him.

A boy I'd known for just twenty minutes but felt I knew him so well, I forgot I didn't even know his name.

A boy who I would never need to flirt with because I could tell he liked me just as much as I liked him.

A boy I would NEVER, EVER, meet again.

And suddenly, on this most exciting day of my entire life, I feel truly, incredibly, stupendously . . . flat.


When I get home I tell Ezzie and Amy all about The Boy On The Train. That's what I call him now. Amy gives me a hug.

'Never mind,' she says. 'Maybe he'll come looking for you one day.'

Some hope!

Back at home life settles into boring routine. The

house is quiet. Ezzie has started to revise seriously for her A Levels and if she's not at college she's poring over physics, chemistry, biology and maths books in her bedroom. Fun! No accounting for taste. I can't wait to do A levels, even though I haven't even started on my GCSEs yet, precisely because it means I can get shot of boring old maths and science and concentrate on interesting subjects like English and drama instead.

How can two siblings be so different?

At school I get mentioned in assembly and have to stand out in front of the whole school and tell them all about the competition, which is mega-embarrassing but I suppose is something I'm going to have to get used to if I'm going to be a television presenter. Anyway, I'm rapidly learning there's no point in being nervous, most people don't listen anyway, because afterwards I get asked questions like 'What's Simon Cowell like?' and 'Did you have to queue up round the block to audition?' like they think I've been on *The X Factor*.

Soon it becomes yesterday's news, which is just as well because, apart from an official letter of congratulations from the television company, I don't hear another thing and I start to worry that I imagined it all and I'm never going to go on the telly after all.

But Mum says, 'Don't fret, they always leave things to the last minute according to Libby,' because now she's in touch with her new best friend, she's all clued up about the world of television. When we got home, she told Grandma and Grandpa all about our surprise meeting up with Libby and Ellie and they were completely dumbfounded, like someone had stopped them in their tracks.

'What's she like now?' asked Grandma in hushed tones.

'Little and skinny with nice straight hair, lucky thing. She's cute, isn't she, Mum?'

Grandma looked confused. The penny drops. 'Sorry,' I said, 'did you mean Libby?'

'No, no, I meant Ellie,' she said, but she was lying, I could tell. And I couldn't help wondering, how weird is that, that it's so long since you saw your own daughter that you have to ask someone else what she looks like?

They'd fallen out, obviously. Libby said as much. Yet they write to each other. And Grandma is so proud of her. I just don't get it.

Since then I've thought about it a lot. I mean, I've met Libby now and she strikes me as a really nice person. I'm no expert on human nature but you can tell, can't you, if someone is genuinely nice or just putting it on to make a good impression? And Libby was kind, it was obvious, just by the way she was with Ellie, and with me too, even though she didn't know me from Adam. She was warm and friendly and she was so concerned when Mum told her about Ezzie.

She didn't seem to be the type to turn her back on her family and her background just because she was famous and successful. I mean, she came all the way out to the hotel to see Mum and me, didn't she, as soon as she knew we were there? She couldn't wait to meet us.

But there was something about Libby that didn't quite add up. For all her smiles and smart clothes, her busy home-life and successful career, I had the funny feeling she was sad. Sorrow hovered over her like a cloud, dimming her natural brightness. She reminded me a bit of Ez who, now she has her own particular cumulonimbus nimbus to cart around, has lost her luminescence too. I'm not calling the baby a cumulonimbus: that sounds like I'm swearing at it! I just mean she's got a cloud above her head too, blocking out the sunshine.

Maybe in Libby's case it's got something to do with the mysterious Sam. Perhaps that's what's kept her away from home for so long.

Anyway, I'm sure I'll find out soon. Mum's been texting and emailing her ever since we got back.

'Libby's sent a reminder to come and stay with her any time we're in London,' says Mum one day when she's checking her messages on the computer.

'What for?' answers Dad tetchily. He's at the kitchen

table filling in another passport form as he can't find the one he did before. Filling in forms is not his favourite pastime but he knows he's got to get a passport soon if he wants to come with me. He's set his heart on me being sent to cover a big football match. I'll laugh my head off if it turns out to be tennis or horse-jumping instead!

'What do you mean, what for?' asks Mum. 'She wants to meet you again, that's what for.'

'I can't see why she suddenly wants to play big sister to me after all these years.'

'It's not just about you,' says Mum frowning. 'She wants her kids to meet their cousins . . . and so do I! *And* I want to meet my all-American brother-in-law, Jay Ryder.' She drawls the last in an unconvincing American accent, trying to lighten the mood, but Dad ignores her and keeps on writing.

'Look,' she says, exasperated. 'I don't know what's gone on in the past, but Libby's offering an olive branch now. The least you can do is meet her halfway.'

'Nothing happened in *my* past!' he says. 'I was just a little kid last time I saw her. I don't know what I could've done to upset her. I can't even remember what she looks like.'

'I reckon she and your parents must have had a falling-out,' says Mum thoughtfully. 'She doesn't include them in

147

this invitation.' She looks up at Dad as he carries on filling in the form, his forehead creased in concentration. 'Martin? What am I supposed to tell her?'

'Tell her what you like,' says Dad moodily. 'D'you know where that flaming certificate is?'

'On the top shelf in the lounge, where you left it,' says Mum and starts tapping out a reply.

'Can you get it for me while I finish this?' says Dad. 'I don't want to miss the post.'

Mum sighs and gets up and goes out of the room. After a while she comes back in, reading the adoption certificate. I expect her to just lay it beside Dad on the table and get back to her emailing, but instead she sits down next to him and studies it intently. I don't think she's seen it properly before. A small frown appears between her eyebrows.

'Martin?'

'What?' Dad's still busy concentrating and is using his leave-me-alone tone.

'Check this for me.'

Something in her voice makes him look up and take the certificate from her outstretched hand without a word. He reads it over and then looks up at her, puzzled.

'What am I looking for?'

'Don't you notice anything odd about it?' she prompts.

He stares at it again, nonplussed. 'What's there to notice?'

'Look at the date of the adoption order.'

He reads it out loud and looks up again. 'What about it?'

'Martin!' Her voice is impatient but gentle at the same time. 'You just don't get it, do you?'

'Get what?' Poor Dad, he's totally bemused. I take the certificate from his hands and study the date.

*I* understand immediately what Mum is going on about.

Dad's date of birth is at the top of the certificate.

His date of adoption is at the bottom.

'You were nearly four years old when this adoption took place,' I say in surprise.

'So?'

'Aren't you curious?' asks Mum. 'Don't you want to find out why?'

'Why what?'

'Why you were that age when you were adopted? Most people are adopted at birth.'

Mum's right. But there's something else too. Something I can't quite put my finger on.

Dad shrugs. 'Not really.'

Mum clicks her tongue, a sure sign she's exasperated. 'I can't believe you don't want to find out more about your background,' she sighs. 'I'm sure you're in denial.'

It's Dad's turn to be cross. 'Denial!' he repeats

scornfully. 'That's just psychobabble! I know I was adopted all right, here's the certificate to prove it.' He snatches it from my hand and waves it in her face. 'But there's no point in raking over old ground, is there? It'll only upset people.'

'Upset who? Liz and Bert, you mean. Well, what about your birth mother, Martin? Maybe she's upset? She's probably out there somewhere yearning for you to get in touch with her.'

'Out there somewhere hoping I never will, more like,' Dad says roughly. 'Come off it, Jo. She must have had a good reason for giving me away in the first place.'

'She might not have,' I say.

'Well, all the more reason for not trying to find her then.' You can tell Dad's getting fed up with this conversation.

'No. I mean she might not have given you away. She might have died.'

Dad and Mum look stunned. Oh flip. That was me being tactless as usual. Mum's hand steals out to enclose Dad's in hers. 'Flick's got a point,' she says gently. 'Maybe that's why you were adopted.'

'Well, in that case, there's no point in looking for her, is there?' Dad says gruffly.

'We don't know for sure though,' Mum persists. 'Can

you remember living with someone else when you were little?'

'No.' Dad looks baffled. 'No, I don't think so. I do have one vague recollection though . . .' His voice tails away.

'What?' ask Mum and I simultaneously.

'It's probably nothing, I haven't thought about it for years. But I can dimly remember being stuck inside a strange house somewhere with a strange woman. I was crying. I didn't want to be there.'

'Perhaps that was her!' I say in excitement.

'No,' says Dad, confused, 'it can't have been. I wanted Mum and Dad, that's why I was crying. I don't know, I probably dreamt it. You know me, I hate being away from home!' He tries to laugh it off but he looks a bit shaken as if the memory has been buried for a long time and now it's resurfaced it's thrown him. 'I honestly can't remember living with anyone else except Mum and Dad. And Libby too, though not so well.'

'I expect she was back and forth to university by the time you were old enough to notice,' says Mum.

'Why don't you ask Grandma and Grandpa, Dad?' It seems so obvious. 'They can tell you.'

'It's not as simple as that,' says Dad, shaking his head. 'They're old. They don't want to be bothered with all this at their age.'

'But you've got a right to know, Dad, you said so yourself,' I protest. Because it's my right as well, it suddenly occurs to me. For all I know, I may have a grandmother out there somewhere and maybe a grandfather too, with a whole set of genes I know nothing about. I mean, look at Ezzie and me, we're chalk and cheese, I'd like to know where we spring from. Mum gets up and puts her arm round me, like she knows what I'm thinking, and we both gaze at Dad pleadingly, as he sits with his elbows on the table, lost in thought, his chin resting on the thumbs of his clenched fists.

'Just ask them, Martin,' Mum urges him. 'See what they think. They might be able to point you in the right direction.'

'Please, Dad.'

There's something niggling in the back of my mind. Something's not right. I don't know what it is. But I do know that it's tied up with Dad being adopted as a little boy.

He raises his eyes to us and sighs heavily. 'Bloody women,' he mutters, and Mum and I grin at each other and give him a hug.

We've won.

Then, being me, I immediately start worrying if we've done the right thing.

★ ★ ★

The next day, after Sunday roast, he puts his jacket on and says, 'I'm popping round to Mum and Dad's to see if they want anything doing,' and I say automatically, 'Wait for me, Dad, I'll come with you,' because Sundays are boring in our house. But Mum frowns at me and shakes her head and Dad carries on out of the door as if he hadn't heard and then I get it. He's off to find out.

Damn, that means I have to give Mum a hand with the washing-up, since Ezzie's having a lie-down in her room. She's getting big now and tires easily. Typically, now it's too late, I wish I hadn't kept on at Dad to have it out with Grandma and Grandpa. I've got them and Grandma Fizz and I really don't need any more grandparents.

But I don't have too much time to fret about this because the next minute there's a knock at the door and I can see Spud's long, rangy figure through the frosted glass, his silhouette, with its outsize dreadlocks, unmistakable. Anyone would think he'd been waiting round the corner till Dad disappeared. Though, actually, now I'm getting to know Spud a bit better, I don't think he'd do that. He's not too fazed by Dad any more. In fact, now I come to think about it, I'm not sure he ever was. Wary, yes; fazed, no. I think it was Dad who was freaked out by Spud.

I'm surprised to see he's clutching a bunch of flowers in his hands, wrapped in newspaper, and I think, ah, Ezzie, that's so sweet (though shame about the wrapping paper) and I wonder if anyone will ever like me enough to bring me flowers. But then he thrusts it into Mum's hands instead and mumbles, 'Purple sprouting broccoli,' at her and she looks as delighted as if he's presented her with a precious orchid. 'Thanks, Spud!' she squeals and to my surprise plants a kiss on his cheek. Spud's face breaks into a wide grin and he bounds up the stairs, two at a time, reaching Ezzie's room without managing to fall over his feet. Mum's eyes meet mine and we giggle and carry on with the washing-up.

Afterwards, Mum settles down with a cup of tea to watch an old weepy movie on the telly. Amy's away for the weekend visiting relatives and there's nothing to do. I wander upstairs to my bedroom and throw myself down on the bed. If Amy does finally manage to go out with Mitch this might be the pattern of things to come. I groan with boredom and turn over, spotting the blue, velvet writing book that Grandma gave me on the shelf next to my bed. I reach for it and open it up, enjoying the smooth, silky touch of the ribbon, and smirk at the picture of Mum asleep with her mouth open on the first page. I never got any further than that, did I? Just a list of the stations we passed en route that day and the clothes that I never wore.

The house is still. From the bedroom next to me, I can hear Ezzie and Spud laughing and then there's silence.

I'm lonely.

I sigh, pick up my pen and continue writing where I left off. Soon I'm lost in my own world, so much so that when the front door bangs, I jump. Dad's home. I finish the sentence I'm scribbling and stare in surprise at the number of pages I've written altogether. Loads! And all of them about The Boy On The Train. No, actually, I suddenly realize, I've written them *to* The Boy On The Train, sharing my thoughts with him. I close the book and place it carefully back on the shelf.

I don't feel quite so lonely any more.

Downstairs Mum and Dad are sitting on the sofa together, looking serious.

'How's Grandma and Grandpa?' I ask, but I can tell from their faces it's not good news. I was right. Dad had gone round there to face them about his adoption. His words are matter-of-fact, like he's come to terms with it. 'I knew it wouldn't work,' he says bluntly. 'They don't want to know.'

Apparently, Grandma had taken it really badly and tried to deny it at first. Then she'd become quite agitated and put her coat on, insisting that she had to go out shopping even though it was Sunday and she had a fridge full of food. Grandpa hadn't been much help either.

'It's all in the past, Martin,' he'd protested when the door had closed behind her. 'Don't go digging it all up again now, it's too late for that. Let it rest.'

Dad had tried to argue with him but he'd been adamant. 'Leave well alone,' he'd said. 'You'll only hurt people with your meddling.'

'Hurt your mother, he means,' says Mum, resting her hand on Dad's. 'He's afraid she'd take it badly if you go looking for your birth mother.'

Dad nods. 'She would. He got all defensive himself after a bit. He kept saying things like, "We did all right by you, didn't we? We gave you everything you wanted. You were happy, weren't you?" like I was accusing him of a miserable childhood.'

'What did you say?'

'I said, of course I was, but they shouldn't have kept it from me. He said, "Aye, perhaps we shouldn't. But we did it for the best." '

Mum strokes his hand. 'What's that saying? The road to hell is paved with good intentions.'

He looks up and catches me taking it all in. 'Blimey, is that where we're all off to? I'm glad I've got my passport then,' he says, trying to laugh it off but it's not funny.

A door opens upstairs and Ezzie and Spud come down. 'What's going on?' asks Ezzie. Mum looks at Dad who looks in turn at Spud and then he shrugs his shoulders and nods. Mum explains what's been going on.

'Poor Dad,' says Ezzie and she perches next to him on the arm of the sofa and strokes his hair. He puts his arm around her and draws her close, his hand resting lightly on the mound of her belly.

'Oh, we'll survive,' he smiles up at her. 'You, me and the little'un here. Life goes on.'

'Grampy couldn't tell you anything about your birth mother?' asks Ezzie.

'Nope,' says Dad ruefully. 'He said he didn't have a clue, they weren't told things like that in those days.'

'I wonder if he's telling the truth?' says Mum thoughtfully.

'What do you mean?'

'Well, think about it. It's very upsetting for them at this stage of their lives, you finding out that you were adopted like that.'

'That's what I told you!' says Dad indignantly but Mum says, 'No, listen. They never told you themselves, did they, so they obviously didn't want you to know in the first place. Years ago, they never expected adopted children to want to trace their birth mothers. Imagine how hard it would be for them now if you find yours. Poor Liz.' Mum looks as if she's going to cry. 'You can't blame them, Martin, for not wanting you to look for her. They've thought of you as theirs all these years. It's the last thing they want now, at their age.'

'Well, that's it then,' says Dad flatly. 'What you're saying is I shouldn't try to find out any more. Which is what I said in the first place!'

'No, I'm not saying that at all,' says Mum. 'I'm just saying, go carefully. And don't expect too much from them.'

'Well, if they can't . . . or won't . . . help, there's not much else I can do anyway,' says Dad resignedly. Then he adds, 'You know the one thing I'd really like to know?'

'What?' we all say in unison, even Spud, who's been taking it all in.

'My name,' he says. 'I've gone through my life so far assuming I'm Martin Pottery. I'd like to know who I really came into this world as.'

I think about it. I guess I know what he means. Like I'm Flick Pottery and my sister's Ezzie Pottery and that's who we are.

At least, that's who we thought we were. In a way this is as important to us as it is to Dad.

'Well, that's easy enough to find out,' says Spud matter-of-factly. 'Just apply for your original birth certificate. It'll be on that.'

'How do you know that?' asks Mum curiously.

Ezzie's cheeks turn a faint shade of pink. 'It's all on the Net,' she says, with a touch of defiance in her voice. 'Under Adoption.'

Amy is doing my head in. She's desperate for Mitch to ask her out and, of course, he hasn't, so now she's decided he's too nervous to make the first move.

'I thought you said he was confident.'

'He isn't actually, Flick, he's quite shy.'

'Mitch? Shy? I don't think so.'

'He is, I've been watching him.' (Well, there's a surprise.) 'He just covers it up well.'

'Extremely well!'

She's not listening. 'I've thought about it a lot and I've made up my mind. I'm going to ask him out myself.'

'Yeah, right.'

'No, I am. I'm serious, Flick. I read an article about it in a mag. It says that girls shouldn't be afraid of making the first move. Boys find it flattering if girls come on to them.'

'I bet they do.' I'm all for equal rights but I have a

horrible vision of Mitch's head getting bigger and bigger as Amy asks him for a date. It'll be all round the school in two minutes and she'll be a laughing-stock. I look at her face, all eager and hopeful. She doesn't deserve that.

*Would you rather Mitch say no and break her heart? Or Mitch say yes and . . . break her heart?*

I'd rather she didn't ask him in the first place. What does she see in him? OK, apart from the obvious, I can't understand why Amy can't see beyond the dark eyes, black spiky hair and wide smile to the loser he really is.

They say love is blind.

Look at Ez and Spud.

Only the funny thing there is, the more I get to know Spud, the more I like him. I used to think that because he worked in the kitchens and didn't say much he was a bit . . . you know . . . thick. But he's not. He's got opinions, more than most, I've discovered, but he keeps them to himself, unless he's asked.

Earlier on this evening, before Amy came around, he was sitting with us in the lounge waiting for Ezzie to get ready upstairs. They were going together to some antenatal class. Mum and I were curled up on the sofa watching telly and Dad was sprawled in his chair next to Spud's, swigging a can of lager.

'What are *you* going for?' asked Dad suspiciously, like he thought Spud had no right to be there.

'To learn how to support Ezzie during labour,' said Spud.

Dad snorted. 'Best leave her to get on with it herself!'

'Like you did?' asked Mum sweetly. She turned to Spud. 'He insisted on being there for the births, then had to leave both times because he felt faint.'

'I want to be there,' said Spud simply.

Dad scowled. After a bit he turned and studied Spud, like he'd never seen him before. It must have been a bit uncomfortable for Spud being scrutinised like that at such close quarters, but he ignored him and carried on watching the news. Then Dad comes out with, 'Do you know, Spud, there's something I've always wanted to ask you.'

'Yeah?'

'What've you got your hair like that for?'

'Martin . . .' said Mum, warningly.

'I mean, no offence, mate,' carried on Dad, regardless, 'but, if you don't mind my saying so, it's a bit . . . crusty, ain't it?'

'Now you're just being rude!' Mum exploded.

'I only asked!' said Dad, acting the innocent.

''S all right,' said Spud evenly. 'Only it's not crusty, man. I keep it clean.'

'Clean!' spluttered Dad, eyeing the ropes of coiled hair hanging round Spud's shoulders. 'Don't look clean to me.'

'Martin!' wailed Mum.

''Tis though,' said Spud as calmly as if Dad had paid him a compliment, not an insult. 'I wash it every night in pure water. No chemicals.'

'More than you do!' snapped Mum, giving Dad a venomous look.

'Do you?' I asked in surprise. 'I thought you had to backcomb it and put beeswax on it to make it into coils.'

'Some people do,' agreed Spud. 'If they wear dreads as a fashion statement. Me, I just let my hair grow in its natural fashion without combing or cutting it.'

'Why?' asked Dad, pointedly.

'Martin!' squealed Mum.

'I don't mind.' Spud turned to face Dad. 'Dreads have been around for thousands of years, Mr Pottery. They have deep religious and spiritual significance, you know; they have links with Hinduism, Islam, Judaism and Christianity. They can also be a political statement or a manifestation of ethnic pride. Nowadays they're associated with the Rastafarian movement which originated in Jamaica in the 1950s. Rastafarians believe in racial harmony and world peace.'

There was silence. This was definitely the longest and most articulate speech Spud had ever made in our company and it didn't sound a bit like him. I got the feeling he was quoting something he'd learned off by heart. It impressed Dad though. He was staring at him open-mouthed as if he'd suddenly grown another head, complete with dreadlocks.

'Right,' he said and licked his lips, like he was having a problem sifting through that much information in one go.

'But,' I pointed out, interested in what Spud was saying, 'you're not Jamaican.'

'*It's not the dread upon your head, but the love inna your heart, that mek ya Rastaman,*' rapped Spud, in a mock-Jamaican accent.

'Cool!' I stared at him in admiration.

Dad stared at him, appalled.

'Sugar Minott,' explained Spud then, seeing Dad's uncomprehending face, added, 'Jamaican reggae singer.'

'Right,' said Dad, totally bewildered by now.

I got the feeling Spud was struggling to keep a straight face. Finally he took pity on Dad and shrugged his shoulders. 'Look, man. I like reggae music. I like to keep my hair free from chemical processing. I like to eat a vegan diet, avoid alcohol and chemical substances and keep my body clean. It's a temple, innit, not a cemetery. Right?'

'Right,' said Dad, who had completely lost the gist of this conversation. He took a swig of his top-strength lager and turned his attention back to the telly, a look of confusion on his face.

'Dead right,' said Mum, looking as if she was trying her best not to laugh.

'Respect.' I added my two-pennyworth. Spud caught my eye and winked.

He's definitely not daft.

Maybe there's more than meets the eye to Mitch too. But if there is, he's hiding it well.

'Do you think I should ask him if he wants to come to the movies with me?' continues Amy. 'There are some good films on. Only that might not be good because we couldn't really talk, could we?'

Something tells me that Mitch, if he agrees to a date with Amy at all, will not be interested in making conversation with her. Not by the way he was eating Zoe that time round the back of the changing rooms, anyway.

'Perhaps I should ask him if he wants to go for a pizza instead.'

'Good idea.' To be honest I'm not really listening. I

keep thinking about Ezzie and Spud. It's really weird to see them going off to antenatal classes together like an old married couple. Soon they'd be a family, mummy, daddy and baby Spud. A new potato.

Only, they're not, are they? An old married couple, I mean. They're young and single; I'm not absolutely sure if they're a couple at all, let alone a married one, though they do seem to be spending more and more time together.

'The thing is, do I pay for him?'

'What?'

Amy's face is anxious.

'Pizza. Do I pay if I've asked him for the date?'

*I want to be there,* Spud had said. *I want to support her.*

Did he mean for ever or just during labour? Spud was a good guy, I was sure of it. He believed in clean living and lots of fruit and veg; he didn't just eat it, for goodness sake, he grew it. *I like to keep my body clean. It's a temple, innit, not a cemetery.* He was more like Grandpa than Dad, he was so straight. He wouldn't abandon Ezzie when she needed him, would he?

A thought occurs to me, leaving me cold. Perhaps Ezzie *didn't* need him after all. Ezzie, with all her plans on hold. Gap year, travelling round the world, working with street kids in South America, university, successful career in medicine. What would she want with a guy like Spud who was content with washing dishes and digging his allotment. Like Grandma said, he could only hold her back.

Maybe she just wanted to have the baby and get rid.

Grandma must've been right after all. Otherwise, why would they be looking up adoption on the internet?

'Oh, this is so complicated,' moans Amy. 'Help me, Flick. Do I pay for him or not?'

'Sorry?' My mind is dragged back reluctantly to the problems of Amy's non-existent love life. 'He should pay. It's tradition. The guy pays on the first date.'

'But I'm breaking with tradition!' wails Amy.

'I don't know. Offer then. If he's a gentleman he won't let you anyway.'

'A gentleman!' She giggles at the archaic word and then her smile fades as it sinks in to both of us that there's no way Mitch would be footing the bill. She sighs heavily. 'I don't know, Flick. Maybe this is not such a good idea after all.'

Thank goodness for that. The penny's finally dropped.

Downstairs the front door slams and Ezzie's voice drifts up the stairs. I open my bedroom door and glance down. She and Spud are back from the antenatal class. As I watch, he bends his head and kisses her gently on the lips. From inside my room I hear Amy's ringtones and her voice rising in excitement as she answers her phone.

Spud helps Ezzie off with her coat and steps back to let her enter the lounge before him.

Now he is a gentleman.

I turn around and go back into my room.

Amy's sitting on my bed, an expression of stunned surprise written on her face.

'Who was that?' I ask.

'Mitch!' she gasps in whispered, reverent tones. 'Flick, I don't believe it! He's just asked me out!'

Dad's got to go for counselling.

It's quite funny really when you think about it. My father is the most down-to-earth, no-nonsense sort of bloke you could ever meet in your life. You should have heard what he had to say about the poor guy he worked with who had time off for stress! Sympathy? I don't think so! He's got no time whatsoever for alternative and complementary therapies and views the people who practise them with huge suspicion. When Mum went to yoga he acted like she was getting involved in some dodgy mystical practice and at the pub quiz he thought shiatsu was a small Chinese dog. He's now convinced that Spud is caught up in some sort of Rastafarian cult, missing the point completely. The chance of him going for counselling was as remote, I would have said, as him opting for colonic irrigation during his lunch-hour.

So what happened?

He did what Spud suggested and applied for his original birth certificate. Poor Dad, he hates filling in forms! Then he was told first of all he should go and see an adoption advisor. So I suppose it's not strictly counselling, though we keep teasing him about it and saying it is. It's advice.

'It's all your fault!' he protests when he gets the letter. 'You were the ones who made me do it.'

It wasn't just us though, he wanted to as well. Like he said, more than anything else he wanted to find out his real name.

But I reckon that's just an excuse. I bet Dad wants to know more than just his name if he's honest. Like, I think he wants to know where he came from. And *who* he came from. I know I would. Only, being Dad, he's just not letting on.

'What do I have to go and see this adoption advisor for anyway?' he scowls, like a kid who's been sent to the head teacher for being naughty.

Mum takes the letter off him and scours it. 'They can help you trace your birth parent and offer you support if you need it.'

'Support!' He spits the word out in disgust. 'I don't need support!'

'It's not just about you,' says Ezzie quietly. 'Years ago people thought once they gave a child up for adoption it was for good. If you do locate your birth mother, it could be a huge shock for her. You don't know how she's going to react.'

I glance at her in alarm. She's obviously thought all this through.

'It happens now too,' I say sharply. '*Some girls* still give their babies away.'

She looks up startled, aware of the edge in my tone that made them sound callous, like their babies were unwanted Christmas presents to be disposed of in a charity shop.

Her cheeks flame but she eyes me squarely. 'It's different now. The birth mother and the adoptive child have rights of their own. If a baby is adopted nowadays they try to keep them in touch.'

'How? How would that work?' I challenge, being as she knows so much about it, but she says, '*I* don't know!' irritably and turns away. I know she's lying.

Mum frowns at me, like I'm the callous one. I'm not the daughter who's considering giving my baby away to strangers! I turn on my heel and flounce out of the room.

Later on, when I've calmed down, I wander upstairs and hang around Ezzie's bedroom by the open door, watching her. She's lying on the bed, studying, her shoulders supported by a cloud of pillows, her book propped up against her belly.

'Go away,' she says, refusing to look up. 'I'm busy.'

*'Would you rather never see me again as long as you live
or see me every day for the rest of your life?'*

'Never see you again as long as I live,' she says, but she
puts her book down.

'Liar.' I throw myself face down on the bed beside her.
'Budge up, Fatty.'

'I'm not fat,' she says moodily. 'Just pregnant.'

'What's it like?' I say, wriggling round and propping
myself up on my elbow to see her.

'Try it and see!' she says, then immediately, 'No, I don't
mean that!' She sighs heavily. 'You wouldn't want to be
pregnant, Flick.'

You bet I wouldn't! But I say, 'Why not?' and reach out
a hand to touch her belly. It feels hard and unyielding.

'Where do I begin?' She shifts position awkwardly.
'Because you look like an elephant; because you feel like
an elephant . . .'

'Elephants are pregnant for eighteen months,' I say,
stroking her belly.

'Poor things,' she says feelingly.

'Kangaroos can keep their pregnancies on hold,' I say,
drawing slow circles on her stomach with the palm of my
hand. 'In times of drought the embryos stop growing
until conditions are more favourable for their survival.'

'How sensible is that?' she says gloomily. 'I wish I could keep this one on hold for the next five or ten years.'

*'Would you rather be pregnant for nine months or pregnant for ten years?'*

'I've changed my mind! Nine months,' groans Ezzie.

'Imagine giving birth to a ten-year-old!' I say with distaste. 'Like Amy's brother. Yuck! It would be cheeky and argue all the time and be obsessed with toilet humour and computer games.'

'I wouldn't want a ten-year pregnancy, that's for sure.' She winces and moves a bit, trying to get comfortable, her belly large and cumbersome. 'I just wish I could delay the whole baby business until I'm ready for it.'

'Won't be long now.'

She sighs heavily. 'No, suppose not. I'm sick of being pregnant but I'm not sure I want it to come yet.'

'It'll come when it's ready,' I say comfortingly, echoing Mum. 'Ouch!' Under my palm I feel a sharp thrust.

'Did it kick you?' Ezzie struggles up on her elbows and pulls her top up, looking down at her belly. It's huge and white with blue distended veins running across it and her belly-button is sticking out like the cherry on top of a bun. 'Grotesque, isn't it?'

I'm about to agree when her belly suddenly ripples, like a wave has passed just under the surface. 'What's it doing?' I ask in awe.

Ezzie grins. 'That's your fault,' she says. 'You've woken it up with all your prodding. It's turning over.' She grabs my hand and presses it hard to the side of her stomach. 'Feel that.'

A sudden, urgent jolt beneath my palm is followed by a second, softer nudge. I take my hand away and watch in surprise as a small egg-shaped mound appears momentarily in Ezzie's stomach then disappears as quickly as it came.

'Wow!' I say, spellbound. 'What was that?'

Ezzie laughs. 'Dunno. An elbow? A foot? A knee? You've got it excited now. It wants to play.'

I press my hand back on the spot and it kicks me obligingly. 'It knows me!' I say delightedly.

Ezzie nods. 'It probably does. They say that babies can recognize voices in the womb. It's bound to know yours, you never stop talking.'

'Yes I do!' I say indignantly, but secretly I'm chuffed. It knows its Aunty Flick. I bend over and press my nose up against Ezzie's tummy and receive a sharp jab in response. 'It kicked me in the nose!' I complain, rubbing it hard, as pleased as punch.

'Don't tease it then!' says Ezzie, her hand caressing,

instinctively, the baby nestling deep inside her womb.

'What are you going to call it, Ez?'

'I don't know.'

'I think you should call it Charlotte if it's a girl or Edward if it's a boy.'

'Mmm. Not sure.'

'Yeah, you have to. Because it's going to be a little spud, isn't it? Charlotte potatoes? King Edwards? Get it?'

'Ha-ha! Very funny. Perhaps we should call it Chips?'

'Chips? I like that! Flick and chips! Hello, Chips. Do you like your new name?' I bend my head down again towards Ezzie's belly and press my lips in a kiss against her white, mottled skin. It could be my imagination but I'm sure I can feel a faint nudge in return. 'He likes it too. Chips it is.'

'You don't know it's a boy,' says Ezzie automatically.

'Doesn't matter,' I say. 'It'll do for now. It should have a name, whatever it is. Names are important.'

'That's what Dad says,' agrees Ezzie. 'He should know. It's the first thing he's had to put down on all those forms he's been filling in.'

'It's the first thing you're asked, wherever you go,' I reflect. '*Name please?*'

'And when you talk about people you say, *He's got a good name*,' says Ezzie, thinking aloud.

'Or, *He's got a bad name.*'

'*It's all in a name.*' Ezzie's getting into the game now, her competitive streak taking over.

'*Named and shamed!*' I say, capping her.

'*Thou shalt not take the name of the Lord in vain!*' she says triumphantly.

I rack my brains but it's no good. 'You win!' I say begrudgingly. 'I can't think of any more. That's a lot though. There's so much bound up in a name, isn't there?'

'It's all about identity. It says a lot about you,' says Ezzie thoughtfully. 'Though I think it was Shakespeare who said, *A rose by any other name would smell as sweet . . .*'

A small switch clicks on in my brain. The Boy On The Train. I can't believe I don't even know his name. And he doesn't know mine . . .

Forget it, Flick. I breathe deeply to get him out of my head and say cheerfully, 'So what's it to be then?'

'What?'

'Chips? Your baby? My nephew/niece? Is he/she going to be a Pottery or a Fernley-Jones?'

Ezzie's face closes over. 'I don't know yet. Nothing's decided. Leave me alone, Flick. I've got to get on with revision.'

My heart lurches. Why does she keep doing this, shutting me out? She can't still be thinking of giving this baby up for adoption, can she? I get up off the bed and go out, slamming the door behind me.

Aunties have rights too!

Life is weird. Why is it that one minute it's really exciting and you're winning competitions and going to television studios and your sister's going to have a baby and you find out your dad's past is far more interesting than you thought it was and you've come across some nice long-lost relatives, and you've found (and lost, boo-hoo!) the love of your life . . . then, suddenly, it's all back to boring old normal again and you start to think you dreamt it all?

Except Ezzie's belly is getting bigger by the day, so I guess that's real enough. She is so fed up with being pregnant now. She's got it into her head she's going to be stuck like this for ever. She hardly ever goes out now her classes are over, she just lies on her bed and revises for her exams. Spud didn't come round for a few days and I started to get worried. In the end I decided to show some sisterly concern and asked her outright if they'd finished. She nearly bit my head off.

'I've got my A Levels coming up, in case you hadn't noticed!' she snapped.

'Sor—ree!' I said, offended, and took myself off to my bedroom and wrote in my book that Ezzie was a moody cow. But then I heard sobbing coming from her room and I got a bit scared and went downstairs and told Mum and she gave me a hug and told me not to worry, Ezzie's hormones were all over the place and she had a lot on her plate and she and Spud were fine.

It's like the whole world is waiting: Ezzie's waiting for her exams to start and her baby to be born; Dad's waiting to hear about his birth certificate and his appointment with the counsellor and it's like, maybe I imagined all that too, because nobody's talking about it; and *I'm* still waiting for Mr Greg Cambriani, Television Producer Extraordinaire, to get in touch with me, only I think he's forgotten I even exist because we've heard zilch from the television studios and I don't care what Libby Ryder, my famous aunt, says, IT'S BEEN A VERY LONG TIME!

Oh yeah, and Amy's still waiting for that date. Mitch may have finally got round to popping the question (all right, asked her to go out with him, but the way Amy goes on about it all the time, you'd think he'd proposed to her), but nothing has actually happened. OK, they do hang out together at break and lunchtime, which personally I find mega-annoying, because Mitch shows off all the time, doing stupid breakdancing routines for some unknown reason and making personal comments about other girls. Amy has developed this really irritating giggle, like she's a tad embarrassed, which is completely understandable. But they haven't been out together in the evening yet, which is what I would call dating.

Amy doesn't seem too bothered when I mention this to her; she seems happy just holding hands with him at school on the rare occasions he's standing still and upright. The worst thing is, she insists *I* hang around with them too.

'I'm not going to dump my best mate, silly, just because I'm dating Mitch,' she says cheesily.

You're not dating, I want to point out, but I keep that fact to myself with a degree of maturity that astonishes me. Amy, sensing my reluctance, steps up the persuasive tactics. 'Mitch really likes you.'

'Does he?' I say in genuine surprise. I assumed my feelings about him were mutual. 'How can you tell?'

Amy is stumped, it's obvious she's made it up. You can almost hear her racking her brain. 'Umm . . . He's got a pet name for you!' she comes up with, at last. 'Nicknames are a sign of affection, my mum says.'

'Really?' I say suspiciously. 'What is it?'

'Fluff.'

'Fluff?' It could be worse, I suppose. 'I'm not fluffy.'

'Your hair is,' points out Amy, helpfully. 'Lovely and fluffy. Like a big marshmallow, Mitch says.'

'Marshmallow,' I say darkly. 'Is that another name of his for me? Very funny.'

'It is, isn't it?' Amy looks relieved. 'I wasn't going to tell you that one in case you didn't like it. Mitch has got such a sense of humour, don't you think? The trouble is, not everyone is on his wavelength.'

'Gosh, I can't believe that!'

'It's true!'

I am *so* fed up.


Grandma and Grandpa come around. We haven't seen them since Dad confronted them about his adoption so Mum invites them for Sunday lunch. It's only a couple of weeks but it's strange, they've changed, they seem older and smaller somehow, especially Grandma. Mum must have thought so too because she says, 'How have you been, Liz?' in a concerned voice as she helps her off with her coat.

'I'm fine.' Grandma's voice sounds the same as usual, so I relax. 'Been keeping myself busy,' she says as she sits down heavily on the sofa. 'These are for you, love.' She hands Ezzie a large brown paper bag.

Inside are three tiny cardigans, one white, one yellow and one green, each with a matching little hat and booties. Mum gasps in delight as Ezzie holds them up to show us.

'Liz, they're beautiful!' she says. 'They must have taken you ages!'

'I'm not as quick as I was,' agrees Grandma. 'I used to be able to run these up overnight for Libby and Martin, but my fingers aren't as nimble as they were.' She looks up at Ezzie and says softly, 'Got to have something nice to bring this baby home in. When we know what it is, I'll do you a pink or a blue one.'

Ezzie leans over to give her a hug, looking as if she's about to dissolve into tears again, which nowadays she does about five times a day. Grandma pats her arm. I can feel myself welling up too. I know what this is. It's Grandma's way of saying, 'Sorry, Ezzie, I was wrong. Keep your baby, it belongs to you. It belongs to all of us.' Only she's knitted the words instead into every perfect stitch, knit one, pearl one, right along each row.

I just hope my sister is listening. What with all those hormones and everything.

Slowly, life shifts back into gear again and lurches unsteadily on.

Ezzie's exams begin.

Amy carries on holding hands with Mitch when he's not writhing about on the floor, king of the Downrock.

I carry on scribbling away in my blue book, trying to keep loneliness from swamping me. Maybe one day my prince will come too. Let's hope he's not quite as into hip-hop as Mitch.

Maybe he's come already only I let him go.

I'm stupid, me. I keep on writing imaginary conversations with The Boy On The Train. It's pointless, I know, I'll never see him again.

I even play Daddy or chips? with him. One day I write:

> Would you rather have loved and lost or never have loved at all?

Isn't that brilliant? Actually, I didn't make this one up. It was from a poem by Alfred Lord Tennyson that we did in school, called 'In Memoriam'. When his friend died he wrote:

> I hold it true, whate 'er befall,
> I feel it, when I sorrow most,
> 'Tis better to have loved and lost
> Than never to have loved at all.

I think that is so beautiful. And so true. I copy it carefully into my book. Then I do a little pen-and-ink sketch of a boy with long hair.

Come on, Flick, be sensible. Nobody's died in your case.

You got on a train.

You met a boy you fancied.

You got off the train.

End of story.

It happens to a million people all over the world on a daily basis.

Get over it.

I can't. It's a bit like picking at a scab. You know you should leave it alone or it won't heal, but you can't help it.

Then one day, Dad takes the afternoon off work to go and see the counsellor. I'd have given anything to have gone with him and so would Mum but he insists on going on his own. I think he's a bit nervous. He doesn't really want to go at all, but it's a legal requirement being as he's applied for his original birth certificate. The trouble is, if it was Mum going, she would have come back and told us everything that went on, but Dad's not like that.

'How did it go?' I ask as soon as he walks in through the door.

'All right.'

I didn't really mean that. I meant:

1. Tell me all about it.
2. What did they say?
3. Do they know who adopted you?
4. Is your birth mother still alive?
5. Why did she give you away?
6. Where has she been all your life?
7. Has she been searching for you over the past four decades?
8. When do we get to meet her?

I open my mouth to ask all these questions but Mum darts me one of her famous looks and I close it again. She goes to the foot of the stairs and calls, 'Ezzie! Tea's ready!' and then says, 'Lay the table, Flick.' By the time my sister's down, Mum's ladling out big bowlfuls of beef stew. She passes one to her but Ezzie screws up her face.

'That's too much,' she says. 'I'm not that hungry.' She looks tired and pale. Mum's about to protest but glances at her and changes her mind. 'Give it to Flick then,' she says and hands her a smaller one.

Thanks, Mum, let Flick get fat instead. Nevertheless, I tuck in obediently.

'How was your exam?' asks Dad and Ezzie says, 'OK,' and Dad nods as if that's all the information he needs. Honestly. You wouldn't want to depend on this family for enlightening and stimulating conversation. I turn my full attention to the beef stew instead, it's far more interesting.

That night, tucked up warm in bed, I hear the murmur of muffled discussion like a buzzing bee coming from my parents' bedroom. It's a comforting sound, droning across my sleepy mind as I drift off. But then I spend the night caught up in a horrible dream where I have to fight off an angry, relentless swarm of bees and I can't get away. I wake up in the early hours of the morning with my legs trapped in a tangle of sheets and the dawning comprehension that Mum and Dad must've been discussing what the counsellor had to say without Ezzie and me being around to overhear.

I draw back the curtains and open my window. The early-morning sun creeps into my room, seeking out the darkest corners, and I look down on the garden, still damp with dew. Summer was nearly upon us and soon it would be full of flowers and those fat, friendly bumble-bees that pollinate them in their striped, furry coats. But I know from my nightmare, you must tread carefully round bees, taking care not to disturb their nest. If provoked, they can give you a nasty sting.

In the cool morning air I shiver and turn away, closing the window behind me. I've got that weird niggling feeling again I've had in the past, ever since we found out Dad wasn't adopted till he was nearly four. Something doesn't add up in all this. What is it?

I go to open my drawer and knock a photo of Ezzie and me off the top of the chest. I pick it up off the floor and glance at it. It's a cute one. Ezzie's about four and she's beaming at the camera, her arms grasped proudly round her baby sister. I'm quite solemn and bald as a coot, just like Dad when he was a baby.

Just like Dad when he was a baby. That's it! That's what's been bugging me all this time. It doesn't make sense. If Dad wasn't adopted until he was nearly four, how come Grandma's got photos of him when he was a baby?

I feel tingly all over. Suddenly, I don't want Dad to go prodding about any more, trying to find out about his past. Because if he persists, he could disturb a hornets' nest and then, who knows? We could all get stung.

I was there when the letter came. We all were. It was half-term for Ez and me, and Mum and Dad had taken the week off too, Mum to do some spring-cleaning, Dad to get various jobs done around the house. Poor Mum, I don't think this was really her idea of a holiday. It seems a long time since she tried to book that fortnight in Spain.

One of Dad's jobs was to clear the small boxroom to make a nursery for the baby. I was really excited about this, not least because it said this baby is here for keeps, so I offered to give him a hand. Somewhere along the line the boxroom had turned into a bit of a dumping ground for stuff we no longer needed but might come in useful in the future.

It was amazing what we found in there, amid all the rubbish. It was a veritable treasure-trove, though how we ever thought we could find another use for this stuff, I have no idea.

Item:

One doll's house (mine). I loved that doll's house! It had a big front door and our cat would squeeze through it if I put some food in there to tempt her. But once she was inside, she couldn't turn round and the whole house would move across the floor like some demented toy from a horror film as she tried to get out.

One toy doctor's set complete with plastic syringe and stethoscope. (Ezzie's, what a surprise.)

One violin. (Ezzie's. She's musical as well as being Brain of Britain. Personally, I think more than one talent is a waste.)

One papier-mâché mermaid, two foot high.

One papier-mâché dinosaur, with flashing eyes. Both of these were class projects made for us by Dad when we were at primary school. Amy was so envious of that dinosaur. I pretended I'd made it myself. I might have fooled Amy but I didn't fool the teacher because she gave Eric Barlow the prize and his dinosaur didn't have any eyes at all, but she said he'd done it all himself and deserved to win. Dad said maybe she'd spotted his style from Ezzie's mermaid a few years before, because teachers have memories like elephants, and he'd have to change his technique next time.

Lots of bin-bags full of fancy-dress costumes, ranging from last New Year's Eve to Reception class.

My mother's creative genius and my grandmother's practical skills stretch back over the years. I can't believe they really dressed Ez and me as two milk bottles and called us The Milk Race. That was tantamount to abuse, that was, stuck inside that cardboard tube. I could hardly breathe and I couldn't see a thing! More bags reveal the Dish and the Spoon (at least I could see this time, even if I was strapped to a four-foot, tinfoil spoon), Two Men in a Boat (I'm sure there were supposed to be three) and The BFG. I got disqualified from that one because I was sitting on Dad's shoulders and even though he was covered up by a huge cape (this time, *he* couldn't see a thing. Revenge!) and there was just my head showing, the teachers sussed it was him underneath and said that parents weren't allowed.

My dad was so competitive! He gets that from Grandma. Mind you, my mum was as bad.

'Someone's having fun.' Ezzie appears at the door. She's been swotting as usual. She leans against the door frame, watching us, her arms folded on top of her belly. Her eyes have dark circles beneath them and she looks exhausted.

'Nearly done,' says Dad cheerfully. 'What colour do you want the room?'

My sister shrugs. 'Dunno. What do you think?'

'Blue,' says Dad.

'Pink,' says me.

'White,' says Mum firmly. She's come upstairs with a letter in her hand. 'That way, when the baby arrives we can accessorise the room in whatever colour you like. What do you think, Ez?'

'Whatever.' Ezzie turns away like she's too tired to care and goes back into her room, shutting the door behind her.

Mum pulls a face. 'She's worn out,' she says, 'what with her exams and everything. Here,' she thrusts the letter into Dad's hand, 'this has just come for you.'

Dad studies the envelope, then pushes it into his back pocket.

'Aren't you going to open it?' asks Mum.

'In a minute!' says Dad, a tad sharply I thought. 'Let's finish the job in hand first.'

I carry the bin-bags full of fancy dress downstairs for recycling and take the opportunity to raid the biscuit tin in the kitchen. Mum calls down, 'I can hear you!' then she adds, 'Make us all a brew, Flick, there's a good girl.' I sigh heavily and put the kettle on. Unpaid labour, that's all I am. I help myself to another biscuit in compensation and wait for the water to boil. By the time I get back upstairs with a tray laden with mugs of tea and the remainder of the biccies, I find Mum and Dad sitting on the floor of the boxroom with their heads together, poring over a piece of paper.

'What have you found? A long-lost will?' I say flippantly, dumping the tray on the floor and squatting down beside them. They look up at me almost guiltily and I spot the open envelope on the floor. My eyes move to the paper Dad is holding in his hand. It looks official. I know what it is. Dad rubs his jaw with the palm of his hand, like he always does when he's bothered about something.

'Nothing to concern you,' he says and starts to fold it up again. Mum puts out her hand to stop him.

'Let her see it, Martin,' she says. 'There've been enough secrets in this family.'

Without a word Dad passes me his birth certificate. Mum scrambles to her feet and yells, 'Ezzie! Come in here, love. You'd better see this too.'

Ezzie comes in with a puzzled frown, takes in the situation and sinks down without a word on the floor beside me. We study my father's birth certificate together. There's not that much to see. Just his date and place of birth, his forenames, Martin George, his sex, and his mother's name. Plus his mother's signature and the signature of the registrar.

That's all.

No father's name.

No father's occupation.

No father.

That's it then. I thought as much. Dad was illegitimate. That's what they used to call it in those days. That's why he was adopted.

Doesn't make any difference, does it? It's still Dad. I look up and shrug my shoulders. 'So?'

'Look at it carefully, Flick,' says Mum.

'What?' I glance back at the certificate confused. 'What do you mean?' I read it again, but I can't see what she's getting at. 'Dad didn't have a father. So what? We'd kind of worked that out, hadn't we?'

'Read the mother's name,' says Mum gently.

'Elizabeth Pottery.' I look up at everyone, still not getting it. 'What's wrong with that?'

'That's Grandma's name,' says Mum and everyone looks at me, even Ezzie, as if that should explain it.

'I know it is!' I say, struggling to see what point she's making. 'I'm not stupid!'

Mum takes my hand. 'This is Dad's birth certificate, Flick. Not his adoption certificate. It contains the name of his birth mother, not his adoptive mother.'

The penny drops. 'Grandma *is* Dad's mother after all?

Brilliant!' I beam at my parents. So that explains why Grandma had photos of Dad when he was a baby. It all makes sense now. 'Dad, you *are* Martin Pottery after all. That's your name!'

Mum and Dad stare back at me solemnly. 'That's good news . . . isn't it?' I ask.

'Well, yes, in a way,' says Dad and he sighs heavily, like he's not too sure.

'But?' There's something not right here. Why isn't Grandpa's name on the birth certificate? I lick my lips which suddenly feel dry. 'Why did they adopt you?' I ask.

'That's what we can't work out,' says Mum.

Finally, Ezzie voices the question I'm dying to ask. 'Does it mean that Grandpa isn't your father?'

'Looks like it,' says Dad shortly.

I stare at him, aghast.

'The father's name and occupation is left empty,' explains Mum. 'If Grandpa was the father his name would be there too.'

'So . . .' I gaze at them all, my confused brain trying and failing to work out the implications of this bombshell. 'What does that mean exactly?'

Mum takes a deep breath, then she says slowly, 'I suppose it means . . . it must mean . . .' She pauses and looks at Dad like she needs help.

Dad shrugs. 'Go on, spit it out.'

'Martin . . .' says Mum, warningly.

'Grandma must have had an affair,' says Dad, his voice harsh.

I gaze at him in horror, shocked to the core.

'Martin,' says Mum in alarm. 'We don't know that for certain.'

'You were the one who said no more secrets in this family!' says Dad crossly. 'Anyway, it's not exactly rocket science. Work it out. My mother had an affair. I was the result. My father, being the good man he is, did the honourable thing and adopted me. End of story.' He laughs bitterly. 'Or it would have been if I hadn't gone poking my nose into other people's business. No wonder they wouldn't tell me anything.'

'NO WAY!' I explode. 'GRANDMA?'

'That's pretty hard to believe,' says Ezzie quietly, looking as dumbfounded as me.

'Is it?' Dad says bitterly. 'People do the strangest things in the name of love, especially when they're young.'

Ezzie's cheeks flush painfully.

I glare at Dad. 'That's stupid! Grandma loves Grandpa! She's always loved Grandpa!'

Dad looks embarrassed.

Mum looks upset.

'Anyway,' I continue triumphantly, 'Grandma wasn't young when she had you, was she? She was over forty, so she couldn't have had some stupid affair!'

Even I know this isn't logical, but I don't care. I'm incensed with rage. How dare my father accuse *my* grandma, his own mother, of having an affair! Of cheating on my lovely grandpa, who is the nicest, kindest, man in the whole world. They love each other! Grandparents don't do things like that! Grandma definitely wouldn't.

*Would she?*

I don't want to think about it, it's too horrible for words. I hate my Dad! Beside me Ezzie gives a little sob and stumbles to her feet. I get up to follow her but I turn as I go out of the room and glower at my Dad.

'I hate you!' I tell him, just in case he's unaware of the fact. I look at my mother, struggling not to cry. 'I hate you too,' I add, almost conversationally, for good measure.

*She* started it all in the first place.

Poor Mum, I didn't mean it. It's not her fault. It's not Dad's either. I come downstairs in the morning ready to apologize to them but they've already gone out.

'Gone shopping, I think,' Spud says. He's sprawled on the floor of our lounge, watching telly. He never sits on a chair if he can help it, he seems more comfortable stretching out on the floor like a big, shaggy dog. I slump into a chair beside him, all churned up inside. Like I say to Spud, I feel really bad now about telling them I hate them and I want to say sorry, but I can't because they're not here, so I'm cross with them all over again.

Spud thinks it's funny.

'That's what families are all about,' he says. 'Shows you all care about each other.'

'How do you work that one out?' I ask grumpily.

Ezzie's ploughing on with her revision upstairs, but she's obviously told Spud all about the argument before she kicked him out of her bedroom. In fact, that's why he probably came round in the first place, like a St Bernard to the rescue.

I must stop thinking of Spud in terms of a large, faithful, untidy dog.

He doesn't think the row is that big a deal.

'If you didn't care, none of this stuff with your gran would matter,' he explains in his flat northern tones. They're surprisingly comforting.

'I suppose so.' As far as I'm concerned, my family's turning out to be a nightmare. I bet Spud had no idea what he was getting himself into when he took up with our Ezzie. I glance at him curiously. 'What about your family, Spud? You've never said anything about them.'

'Not much to say.'

'Tell me!' He's so infuriating! If I asked Amy to tell me about her family, she wouldn't stop talking for a fortnight. 'What's your mum like?'

'Bit of a hippy. Or she was when I was growing up. She lives in Spain now. She went there when I was fifteen. I had to go with her, that's why I never did my exams. But I came back a year later. I didn't think much of it, where she is, not my scene. I prefer it here.'

Wow! Long speech, Spud.

'What about your dad?'

'Never really knew him, he wasn't around much. They

weren't married. That's why I was called Alastair Fernley-Jones. My mum's name was Fernley, my dad's, Jones.

'Brothers and sisters?'

'Not that I know of. It's possible though.' He grins. 'Anything's possible.'

Don't I know it.

'Doesn't it bother you, being on your own?' I couldn't imagine not having family around. No Mum or Dad. No Ezzie. No Grandma or Grandpa.

Only I guess, strictly speaking, Grandpa's not officially family any more.

I can't believe that.

Spud thinks for a minute. He's like that, I've noticed. He weighs things up before he answers, not like me who blurts things out without thinking and then regrets it. I stir uneasily. Where have Mum and Dad got to? They've been gone ages. I've been horrible to them. I don't really hate them. I was just upset about Grandma.

'It's got its advantages,' he says finally. 'You don't have any expectations on you, so you can just be yourself.'

I nod. 'I know what you mean. Like Grandma, she's really keen on us to do well. She goes on about it all the time.'

'That's good,' says Spud. 'She's just encouraging you. No one ever encouraged me.' He says this without a trace of self-pity, then he adds, 'She's all right, your grandma.'

'I know that!' Spud doesn't have to defend Grandma to me, I know what she's like better than he does.

At least, I thought I did.

Anyway, if he knew what she'd said about him, he might not be so keen to spring to her defence. I think about the day Grandpa told her off, warned her to stop interfering in other people's lives. 'It's just that she doesn't like things getting in the way of our futures.'

'Like Ezzie getting pregnant, you mean?' He's a mind-reader. I shrug my shoulders, not knowing what to say. 'Well, that's understandable, you can't blame her for being worried.'

I shake my head. This guy is something else. 'Don't you ever get cross about anything?'

Again, he considers the question. 'Yeah,' he says finally.

I wait impatiently. 'Like?'

'Global greed. Third World poverty. Hunger. War. Disease. Waste. Destruction of the planet . . .'

'Blimey, Spud!'

'You asked!' he says mildly then adds, 'Cheeky kids who hate their parents . . .'

'I don't!' I glance at the clock uneasily. 'I wonder where they are? They've been gone ages.'

A tiny sliver of fear shafts itself through my heart.

When I was little and got told off I used to get in a right paddy, I couldn't help it, and I'd scream and shout at Mum or Dad and get sent to bed. But I could never be angry for long. Instead, I'd lie awake, terrified that they would die before I could say I was sorry.

I'm still a bit like that now.

A key turns in the lock and the front door opens. I jump to my feet, expecting Mum to call out, 'Give us a hand with these bags!' but instead they make straight for the kitchen. I follow them in. There are no bags, they haven't been shopping at all. Dad chucks his keys on the worktop and picks up yesterday's paper. Mum grabs the kettle and twists the tap sharply and the water spouts everywhere. No one says a thing but you could cut the tension with a knife.

'Where've you been?'

Mum darts a look at Dad. He's sat down at the table, his head in the paper.

'Grandma's.' She plugs the kettle in. 'Coffee?'

'No thanks.' I watch as she busies herself with mugs, coffee, milk. 'Sorry, Mum.'

She looks at me blankly. 'What for?'

'For saying I hate you. I don't, by the way. Nor Dad.'

'Of course you don't.' She pours the boiling water into the mugs, whisks them briskly with a spoon and bangs one down in front of Dad. Then she sits down opposite him, nursing her steaming mug in her hands.

'How's Grandma?'

Mum's lips tighten. 'We've had a row.'

'Why?'

'Why do you think?' She sighs and puts down her mug. 'We wanted to talk to her about your dad's birth certificate but they didn't want to know. They got really upset. Grandpa told us to go.'

'Did he?' I'm shocked. Grandpa's the mildest-mannered man I know. Except for Spud.

'I told you this would happen,' says Dad gruffly.

'They refused to talk about it,' says Mum and she looks really angry. 'What really bugs me, Martin, is the lies they've told you. Your father said to you before that they didn't know who your birth mother was and it was her all the time!'

'He was trying to protect her,' says Dad and lays down his paper. It's obvious he's not reading it anyway, he's just trying to escape Mum who's like an irate tiger defending her cub. 'Give them a bit of time, they'll come round.'

'No they won't! They'll just bury it under the carpet again and pretend it never happened. You've got a right . . .'

'Give over going on about my rights!' he snaps and gets up from the table, knocking his chair over in the process. 'I'm sick of you banging on about it. Stop your yacking for one minute, woman, and listen to what my father said! LEAVE WELL ALONE!'

He stalks out of the front door, banging it shut behind him. From upstairs Ezzie shouts, 'What's going on down there?' Mum bangs the table with her fist in frustration.

'Grandma and Grandpa won't talk to them about the adoption,' I explain to Ez who's appeared at the kitchen door. Behind her is Spud who must have heard it all from the lounge.

'They're all as bad as each other, those flipping Potterys,' says Mum. 'Why all the blooming mystery, I'll never know.'

'Well,' says Spud slowly, sitting down beside her, 'maybe there's nothing else to talk about. You know who the mother is. You know Liz and Bert stayed together and brought Martin up as their own. What else matters?'

'Plenty, if you must know!' says Mum, rather childishly I thought. She gets like this when she's in a tizz. 'Who's the father, for one thing? And why did they wait four years to adopt him, for another? Why did they bother to adopt him at all, come to that? They could've passed him off as Bert's, nobody would have been any the wiser.' She gives Spud a sour look, as if to say, what's it to do with you anyway? 'We can never get answers now, that's for sure.'

'Yes you can,' says Spud, not looking a bit put out by

Mum snapping at him. 'That's easy to find out.'

Three pairs of eyes stare at him in surprise.

'How?' asks Ezzie.

'Ask Libby.'

Spud is Albert Einstein and Stephen Hawking rolled into one.

It's like everyone's been buzzing round in all directions, like crazy bluebottles, asking questions and creating lots of noise but getting nowhere, and he's quietly zoomed straight to the answer.

There's a stunned silence then Mum says, 'Libby?'

'Ezzie said there was a big age gap between her and her brother,' explains Spud. 'So she'd remember it all, wouldn't she? She could tell you what happened.'

'Why didn't I think of that?' breathes Mum.

'How much older is she than Dad?' I ask.

'Quite a bit. Seventeen years, I think. By the time he was old enough to remember her, she was at university and he only saw her in the holidays. Then she went to live in America for years. Like he said, he hardly knew her.'

'But she'd remember him being born, wouldn't she?' says Spud logically.

'Yes, she would.' Mum beams at us all and suddenly she springs to her feet. 'You're a genius!' she pronounces. She pinches Spud's cheeks and plants a big smacker of a kiss on his forehead. 'Uggh!' she adds as she bounds out of the room. 'When are you going to get that hair of yours cut?'

'Cheek!' Ezzie splutters but Spud looks pleased.

I don't think anyone's ever called him a genius before.

Amy comes over on Friday and we go round to see my grandparents. I hate what's been going on, it's made me feel awkward with them; I've been avoiding them a bit because I'm not sure how much they think I know. But when Amy suggests that we pop in to see them on the way to town, I jump at the chance, because if she's with me it makes everything normal again. She loves going to their house.

'They're proper grandparents, aren't they?' she witters on as we walk there together. 'Like your gran knits and makes cakes and your granddad gardens and plays bowls. I wish mine were like that. My nana's still working and she says she hasn't got time to make cakes.' She pulls a face. 'It's just an excuse, I don't think she's ever made one in her life. And if my granddad's not playing with his Xbox, he's on Facebook all the time. He wanted *me* to be his friend!' She shudders.

'I know what you mean,' I laugh. 'Grandma Fizz is the same. She's always out. She goes salsa-dancing and plays badminton and when Mum said, poor old thing, she'd better invite her down for Christmas last year or she'd be on her own, Grandma Fizz said, no thanks, she'd booked to go to the Maldives with a friend. Mum was green with envy! She says there's no stopping her since she's been on HRT.'

'It's not right though, is it?' says Amy, shaking her head in disapproval. 'Facebook and salsa-dancing and that. Grandparents aren't what they used to be. If only they could all be like yours and act their age. Make jam and cakes and that. Definitely cakes. You'd know what to expect then.'

Actually, I don't know what to expect from my grandparents any more, but I don't think I should enlighten her on that score so I just mutter modestly, 'Well, they're getting on a bit,' and bask in her approval. And when we turn up at their house it's like they know they've got a reputation to live up to because Grandpa's on his knees in the front garden putting in some bedding plants and he sits back on his heels when he sees us and tips his cap back.

'Hello, girls,' he says, 'must have known you were coming, Grandma's made a cake,' and Amy grins at me in delight. When we step inside, the whole house smells of baking and she nearly faints with pleasure.

Grandpa's come in from the garden to join us and we're all sitting round the table tucking into tea and fruit cake when the phone rings.

'It's for you,' says Grandma, holding the phone out towards me. 'It's your mother.'

'She probably wants me to fetch her something from town,' I grumble and grab another big bite of cake before I take the phone from her.

'Yes?' I mumble indistinctly.

'Flick?' Mum's voice is high and squeaky with excitement. 'Greg Cambriani's just phoned.'

I gasp in surprise, because, honestly, I'd practically given up on him. Unfortunately, I've forgotten my mouth is full of cake, which is sucked into my windpipe and I start to choke. Amy gets up and thumps me helpfully on the back and I cough up bits of sultanas, currants and raisins as she takes the phone from my hand and listens to my mother's news first-hand. She assures her that no, I'm not choking to death and yes, she will tell me the good news, and then she places the receiver back into its cradle and does a weird dance, treading my cake crumbs into the carpet and shrieking her head off.

'You lucky thing!' she yells, her arms flailing about, then sings tunelessly, 'Lucky! Lucky! Lucky!'

'What?' I ask in strangled tones, battling to get my

breath back as my grandparents look on in consternation, though whether they're more bothered about my welfare or their carpet, I can't tell.

'You're only off to Italy!' she whoops. 'To report on the Champions League Final for children's television! Go Flick! Go Flick! GO! GO! GO!'

Amy and I never got to town that day, needless to say. It was straight back round to my house to find out all the details.

'Jump in the car,' says Grandpa. 'We'll give you a lift.'

But Grandma says, 'You take them, I've got a bit to do here,' and she starts collecting up the cups and plates. I say, 'Leave those, Grandma, we'll do them. Go and get yourself ready,' but she flaps her hand at me and says, 'No, no, you go. I've things to get on with.' I feel sad then because not so long ago, when she heard I had an audition, she was round my house at the speed of lightning, wild horses wouldn't have kept her away.

I feel worse when Grandpa drops us off and won't come in. 'Got to get back,' he says, looking like he doesn't want to at all. 'Must finish getting those plants in.' Like it would make a blind bit of difference if those plants had to wait another ten minutes. I know it's an excuse and so does he, because he looks miserable as he drives away which makes me unhappy too.

But then the front door opens before Amy and I get to it and Dad comes out whooping his head off and picks me up in his arm and swings me around, like a little kid. The next-door neighbours are in the garden and they ask what's going on and the next minute the news is flying around the neighbourhood, and soon there's a stream of women and kids and the odd dad turning up to find out if it's true that I'm going on the telly.

Mum puts Amy and me in charge of tea and biscuits while she regales everyone with the details and Dad cracks open a can and boasts that he's off to the Champions League Final. Soon Ezzie gives up any attempt at revision and comes downstairs to join the throng and immediately the talk turns to childbirth as every mother in the room competes to tell the story of who had the most traumatic time in labour. Amy looks decidedly queasy. It's enough to make your hair curl, though not mine of course, because a) I've already heard Mum's accounts of Ezzie's and my birth in far too much detail and b) it's already like a corkscrew.

Spud turns up in the middle of it all and Dad thrusts a celebratory can in his hand. I'm not sure what's happened to his 'My body is a temple' philosophy: hang around with Dad much longer and he'll be a raging alcoholic. Looking at Spud, the women's conversation changes to dreadlocks and then tattoos and piercings in unlikely places, which proves far more entertaining than childbirth, though it makes me think twice about having something stuck into my skin, I can tell you.

With all this going on, I don't have time to dwell on my grandparents' absence from the proceedings. Later on, when everyone's gone and all the excitement has died down, I sit down with my parents.

'Peace at last!' says Mum with relief.

Dad snaps open yet another can. 'You'd better get used to this, Flick,' he says, taking a swig. He licks his lips and belches smugly. 'This is just a foretaste of what's to come now you're a celebrity.'

'Flick being a celebrity doesn't mean *you* have to keep on celebrating!' says Mum, whisking the can from his hand. 'We've got to put the recycling out tomorrow. I don't want those binmen thinking we're boozers!'

The television company have said if we want to, they'll fly Dad and me out to Italy two days early so we can acclimatize ourselves before the Final.

'Not fair, is it?' declares Mum for the umpteenth time. 'Who's been trying to get a holiday abroad for the past twenty years? Me. Who gets to swan off to Italy with you, all expenses paid? Your father.'

Dad doesn't offer to give up his place to Mum. I don't think she really minds though; she's just enjoying going on about it.

Suddenly she sits bolt upright.

'I tell you something they haven't thought of,' she says. 'You'll need somewhere to stay in London the night before.'

'That's all right,' says Dad expansively. 'Greg'll take care of it.' Greg, as in, Greg Cambriani, TV bigwig. Dad's new best mate.

'No need!' says Mum, springing up from her chair. 'Libby will put you up. She's always asking us to come to stay. I'll email her now.'

'I'd rather stay in a posh hotel!' protests Dad, but Mum's not listening.

'I want to tell her about Flick anyway.' She logs into her emails. 'She's bound to want you to stay with her when she knows you'll be in London overnight.' She scans quickly through her inbox, looking for Libby's name amidst the forest of adverts for holidays that she's been deluged with ever since she tried to book herself one. 'That's funny, I thought I would've heard from her by now. She hasn't got back to me yet about your adoption.'

'Perhaps she's away,' suggests Dad.

'You can access your emails anywhere,' says Mum, as if

he's the one person in the twenty-first century unaware of this. 'You don't have to be at home.'

'Is that a fact?' asks Dad and winks at me. 'Well I never! I thought that was only if you had a laptop.'

'No, you can do it on a PC,' says Mum, taking him seriously. 'That's what they have internet cafés for. Though,' she looks a bit worried, 'maybe she's somewhere far away where they don't have the internet.'

'Www dot . . .' I hint.

'What?'

'World wide web? Get it?'

'I see what you mean. Anyway, she'd be bound to have her laptop with her, she's in television.' Mum taps out a message to Libby, who's obviously wandering around some far-flung rainforest with her laptop under her arm and presses Send. 'There you are. She should get back to me pretty soon, if I know Libby. Funny that. She didn't say she was going away.'

'Maybe she doesn't tell you everything,' says Dad, getting bored with the conversation. 'You don't know her that well, Jo, you've only met her the once.'

Mum looks a bit put out. As far as she's concerned, she and Libby are bezzies. Dad pushes home his advantage. 'I'll ask my mate Greg to book us a nice hotel, hey, Flick?'

My mate Greg? My bestest friend Libby? Since when

did my parents start hobnobbing with television producers and directors?

'Hold your horses,' says Mum shortly. 'We'll wait to see if we hear from Libby first. I've asked her now.'

In the end, Dad gets his own way. Mum checks her emails every five minutes for the next few days but it does start to look as if Libby's vanished off the face of the earth.

'She could've told me she was going away,' says Mum, fuming with frustration.

'She was always a funny one,' says Dad. 'She disappeared from our lives for years, remember. A leopard doesn't change its spots.'

'I thought she was nice,' says Mum regretfully. 'She seemed as if she wanted to get to know us all.'

'Well, she's not answering your messages,' points out Dad. 'And we need to get some accommodation sorted out. We're going soon.'

'I'd give her a ring,' says Mum. 'But I don't know what I've done with her phone number.'

'Greg'll have it,' I say and Mum beams at me.

'Of course he will.' She makes straight for the phone and dials the number.

'Greg?' Her face lights up. 'Jo Pottery. Hi. Good, thanks.' She witters on for a bit then gets down to business. 'We're trying to get hold of Libby and we were wondering if she was away.' I can hear Greg jabbering at the end of the line. Mum's face darkens. 'No,' she says decisively, 'I don't need her mobile number. It doesn't matter, it wasn't important. Martin wants a word with you, by the way.' She pushes the receiver into Dad's hand. 'Book your flaming hotel!' she mutters bitterly. 'Sod Libby.'

'What's up?' I whisper but she shakes her head and waits till Dad's finished on the phone before she says indignantly, 'She's been there all the time, working in the studio next door to him.'

'Sounds like she's been busy,' Dad says diplomatically.

'Busy, my backside!' she explodes. 'She just doesn't want to put you and Flick up at her house and she's too rude to let us know. Now I feel really stupid for asking. I wouldn't mind, but she was the one who invited us in the first place!'

'People often say come and stay but they don't mean it,' says Dad wisely, like he's suddenly developed a white beard and a membership to Mensa.

'She meant it,' I say, puzzled. 'She said they had plenty

of room.' Libby seemed really sincere to me. I remember how concerned she was about Ezzie and how I'd wondered if there was something going on with her own son, Sam, because she seemed sad, underneath the effervescence. Maybe he'd been up to something again. 'Perhaps something's happened?'

Mum sniffs. 'Who knows? If she can't be bothered to get back to me, I don't care. She's changed her mind about keeping in touch, that's obvious.'

Poor Mum. She does care. She seems really upset, like I am on the rare occasions Amy and I fall out. 'Well, I won't be bothering again, that's for sure,' she adds emphatically.

Pity. I really liked Ellie and I'd been looking forward to meeting the mysterious Sam.

I really liked Libby too.

Sometimes you can be so wrong about someone. I put my arm around Mum and give her a squeeze.

*'Would you rather, come with me and Dad to Rome to watch the Champions League Final or go and stay at Aunty Libby's poncy house in London?'*

Not a good choice. Mum hates football. Upstairs a door opens and we hear Ezzie padding heavy-footed down the stairs. Mum gives a wry smile.

'Neither,' she says. 'At this moment in time, I'd rather

218

stay put and keep an eye on Ezzie.'

'You've got to choose!' I insist but Mum's not playing. She shakes her head. 'Won't be long now.'

'She won't have the baby while we're away, will she?'

'I shouldn't think so,' says Mum, but when we turn to look at Ezzie as she enters the room, I'm not convinced. My sister looks about to burst, her skin stretched taut and tight round her blown-out belly. She reminds me of that beautiful golden flower Grandpa grew once in his greenhouse. He explained to me that once its seeds were mature, its sac would explode and expel them into the air. Just a slight tap would set it off, which is probably why it was called 'Touch-me-not', if I remember rightly. Ezzie looks like one little touch would set her off too.

'Don't you dare give birth while I'm away in Rome!' I say fiercely.

She looks at me in surprise. 'I can't,' she says simply. 'I've got my exams to get through first.'

But that doesn't reassure me. I'm not stupid, I know that babies come when they want to. Ezzie sinks into the chair and sweeps her hair back from her brow. Everything about her is weary. For the first time since I heard the exciting news that I was off to Italy, I wish I wasn't going.

I hate men. They are so not worth it. Amy's in bits and it's all stupid Mitch's fault. First day back at school after half-term, he's only gone and dumped her.

He's been using her to get at Zoe, I reckon. He's always fancied her. I think he asked Amy out just to make her jealous. But now she's going out with a Year 11 and Mitch can't compete with that, so he's given up on her and has no more need of Amy. That's my theory anyway.

Of course that's not what Mitch said.

'He says he really likes me, but he's not looking for a long-term relationship,' explains Amy tearfully.

'Why not?'

'He says he needs to find himself first.'

Huh! 'Well that makes sense,' I agree. 'He's a loser so he'd need to find himself, wouldn't he?'

Wrong tactic. 'He's not a loser!' snaps Amy, springing immediately to his defence. 'He's kind . . . and

sensitive . . . and generous . . . and soooo good-looking!'
The last ends on a wail.

Mitch, good-looking? Unfortunately, yes, in a toxic
sort of way. Kind and sensitive? I don't think so.
Generous? Come on, Amy, you never even had a proper
date, he was too tight to take you out. I'm just about to
point all this out to her, thinking it might help to have a
more objective point of view, when Spud remarks mildly,
'He's probably just not ready to commit.'

It's nearly teatime. Mum's in the kitchen cooking and
Spud is in the lounge with us, waiting for Ezzie to come
back from college. She's sat her last exam today! Poor Ez.
All her mates will be out tonight, celebrating the end of
A Levels, and she's just about ready to pop. 'It's not your
fault,' continues Spud. 'Sounds to me like he's still got a
bit of growing up to do. Boys aren't as mature as girls.'

You can say that again. Though there's always an
exception to the rule. When I look at Spud I wonder if
he was ever a kid or if he was born into this world with
dreadlocks, a love of the planet and more wisdom, I'm
beginning to realize, than anyone else I know. I suppose
you've got to grow up fast if you've been on your own
since you were sixteen.

Amy sniffs and nods solemnly in agreement. 'I think
maybe you're right,' she admits. 'Mitch could be
immature at times.'

I gasp. Isn't that what I've said all along? I could have saved her all this heartache and me all this earache if she'd only listened to me in the first place.

I'm learning fast here. When it comes to friends who've been dumped, say nothing, hand out tissues and give lots of hugs. The last thing they want is for you to point out the obvious to them . . . that they've been wasting their love on a sad, bad loser. Still, I can't resist one last jibe.

'Look on the bright side, Ames. At least you won't have to spend lunchtimes watching him break-dancing any more.'

For a nanosecond she looks annoyed but then her face splits into a grin.

*'Would you rather have a gorgeous boyfriend who dances rubbish or a rubbish boyfriend who dances gorgeous?'*

'A gorgeous boyfriend who dances rubbish,' I say automatically and then realize it's the wrong answer as I watch her face fall again. 'What do I know?' I say wildly. 'I've never even had a boyfriend! At least someone's liked you enough to ask you out!'

'Aah,' says Amy, putting her arm around me, 'don't worry, Flick. Someone cute like Mitch will turn up for you one day.'

Puh-lease! I sincerely hope not! As if on cue, the

front doorbell rings.

'Here he is now,' giggles Amy. 'Go and let him in, Flick.'

'No!' I say, pretending to be scared. 'I can't! You go!'

'No, you go!'

'I'll get it!' says Spud. 'Idiots!'

When he opens the door we hear a deep, male voice. Amy and I glance at each other in shock and then we both start to laugh. 'I told you!' she says and simultaneously we both spring to the door of the lounge to listen in to the conversation. The voice has got an accent. An American twang.

'Who is it?' I mouth at her.

'I ordered a boyfriend for you off eBay!' she whispers back. 'They must have sent it from America.'

Laughter bubbles up inside me and I grip my nose tightly to stop it coming out. Amy's eyes are round with excitement and she looks really comical.

'It's probably the Mormons!' she says and it's no good, I start spluttering. The door opens wide and knocks us both off balance and we fall backwards on to the floor. Spud looks down at us in surprise.

'Someone to see you,' he says.

A tall, well-built figure fills the doorway. My first thought, bizarrely, is he's too old for me; my second, even more incongruous, is, pity, he's good-looking in a lined, middle-aged, crumpled sort of way. He's wearing jeans and a T-shirt and one of those light linen jackets that look permanently creased, and his face is creased too, with amusement, as he looks down at Amy and me spread-eagled on the carpet.

'Hi,' he says, in a deep American drawl. 'Which one of you ladies is Elizabeth and which is Felicity?'

I scramble to my knees, trying to rescue some dignity from the proceedings. 'I'm Felicity. Flick, that is. This is my friend Amy.'

'Good to meet you, Flick. I'm Jay. Jay Ryder.' He thrusts out his hand and takes mine in a strong, firm grip. 'Here, let me help you.' He hauls me to my feet then does the same for Amy.

'You're married to my Aunty Libby!' I say and his eyes crinkle up even more.

'I do believe I am!' he says. 'I've got someone with me whom I think you know.'

A beaming face framed by a neat, shiny bob pokes out from behind his bulky frame. 'SURPRISE!'

'Ellie!'

My cousin launches herself at me, squeezing me round the waist in a big bear hug. I throw my arms round her in delight.

'Mu-um!' I yell. 'Look who's here!'

The kitchen door opens and Mum appears, looking a

bit taken aback at the throng in her hallway, until she spots Ellie and then there's lots of squealing and hugging and introductions and handshaking.

'What a lovely surprise!' says Mum, when we've all calmed down a bit and we're sitting round the kitchen table with a cup of tea. 'Where's Libby?'

'We've left her catching up with her parents,' explains Jay. 'She wanted to have a bit of a chinwag with them on her own.' He raises his eyebrows meaningfully at her.

'They didn't tell us you were coming,' says Mum, puzzled.

Jay shakes his head. 'They didn't know. We decided to come on the spur of the moment. Libby enjoyed meeting you so much, she was determined to keep in touch. Then she got your email about Martin's adoption and well, to be honest, it threw her a bit. We talked it over and decided she really needed to come down here and speak to you in person. So we got in the car and here we are!' He grins at us cheerfully as if he couldn't imagine anywhere else he'd rather be. 'We don't want to put anyone to any trouble. We've booked into a hotel in town for a few nights.'

'Well, you can just unbook!' says Mum firmly. 'You're staying with us.'

'Actually, there are probably too many of us to do that,' says Jay. 'We've got Sam with us too. He'll be here in a sec. He's just popped into the shop on the corner to top up his phone card.'

A small thrill of excitement courses through me. This is too much! Bad Boy Sam! I get to meet you at last. I remember Ellie's words, 'Sam's *in luurve!*' and I think, I bet he's topping up his card to chat to his girlfriend. I turn to Amy in excitement. 'Sam's my cousin. He's seventeen.'

Amy's eyes flicker with interest then suddenly she looks at her watch and groans. 'I've got to go. Mum says if I'm late for tea again I'm grounded.'

'I'll see you out.'

At the front door, Amy says, 'Jay is so cool. Why isn't my Uncle Fred like that? He's fat and ugly and he keeps on asking me when I'm going to get married. I *think* he's joking.' She looks a bit sad for a minute so I give her a hug.

'Don't worry about Mitch,' I say. 'Plenty more fish in the sea.'

'Yeah, you're right,' she says, giving me a brave little smile. 'There are trillions of boys dying to go out with me. I just need to cast my net a bit wider.' She peers short-sightedly at a boy sloping up the street towards us, his hands in his pockets. 'He'll do. I wouldn't mind catching him.' Then she looks at her watch and gasps. 'Is that the time? Got to dash!'

She careers off down the street, almost bumping into

the boy, whether by accident or design it's hard to tell. He veers to one side and turns to watch her for a second, then continues on his way, glancing up at the houses as he passes as if he's checking the numbers. There's something familiar about him.

He's tall and he's wearing dark blue jeans, a green T-shirt and a beanie which doesn't quite hide the sun-streaked hair beneath. When he spots me standing in the doorway he stops and says, 'Excuse me, can you tell me where . . . ?' But then his jaw drops open mid-sentence and his blue-grey eyes widen in surprise.

Then they crinkle up, just as I remember, and he says, 'Hey!' at the same time as I say, 'You?'

'Great hair!' he adds and, self-consciously, my hand moves up to touch it. I remember, the last time we met, it was tucked inside a beanie.

'Thanks.' We stand there grinning at each other inanely, while the sun comes out and lights up the street and my heart soars up to greet it.

This is the most romantic thing that has ever, ever, happened to me.

He's come to find me.

The Boy On The Train.

'It's you!' he says.

I nod.

'That's unbelievable!'

I nod again, not trusting myself to speak.

'I never thought I'd see you again.'

I think I'm going to die with happiness.

'Me neither.'

'Do you live here?'

'Yeah.'

He must think I'm a total idiot. He's come all this way to find me and all I can do is nod my head and say, 'Yeah'! Say something quick.

'It's like a book,' I say, then immediately wish I hadn't, but it's OK because he says, 'Or a film. One of those musicals where they start dancing in the street.'

'Like *Grease*!' we both say at the same time and laugh.

'We just need some cars to dance on,' he adds.

'Plenty of those.' I indicate the cars parked bumper to bumper on the road. It's just like it was on the train. He's so easy to get on with.

'How did you know where to find me?' I ask.

'I didn't. This is like, crazy! I had no idea you lived here.'

The sun moves behind a cloud, leaving the street suddenly cold. I shiver and rub my arms with my hands. Something's not right. If he'd come looking for me . . . why was he so surprised to find me?

'What number is this?' he asks suddenly.

'Twenty-eight.'

'Twenty-eight?' he echoes and looks away down the street frowning, like he's trying to work something out. Then he looks back at me and he's different somehow. The light has gone from his face, leaving it blank. 'Is your name Flick by any chance?' he asks.

'Yes.'

'Flick Pottery?'

'How do you know my name?'

He breathes out, a long, slow breath like a sigh.

'That's unbelievable!' he says, for the second time, but now it brings a chill to my heart.

He's silent for a second then he says abruptly, 'My mum's Libby.'

'Libby Ryder?'

'Yes.'

My brain starts whirling madly like someone's spun a coin inside my head.

'You're Sam!'

'Yes.'

Bad Boy Sam.

The Boy On The Train is Bad Boy Sam.

The coin spins crazily, colliding with my hopes, knocking them flat.

'You're my cousin?'

'Looks like.'

Everything is still.

I don't know what to say.

I don't know what to do.

Sam straightens his shoulders and thrusts out his hand. 'Good to meet you, Flick. I've heard all about you.'

His voice is different now. Impersonal, as if we've just been introduced. I shake his hand numbly. Start again. That's the way it has to be now. He's my cousin, for goodness sake.

'Likewise.' I feel such an idiot.

The Boy On The Train.

Over the past few weeks he'd achieved iconic status in my life.

I'd thought about him in capital letters.

I'd thought about him all the time.

I'd talked to him in my diary.

I'd thought we'd got on so well.

I'd thought he felt the same.

I'd totally convinced myself we were meant to be together.

I'd thought one day he might come looking for me.

Then we would live happily ever after.

I'd told myself this every day, on my way to school, in boring maths, when Amy was bleating on about Mitch, before I went to sleep at night.

In your dreams! Wake up, Flick. You've been reading far too much chick-lit, that's your trouble. Romantic love is the stuff of myths and fairy tales and musicals like *Grease*. In real life it doesn't work out like that.

'You were looking for your father and your sister?' My voice is polite and strained.

'I guess.'

A hot wave of embarrassment engulfs me and I start babbling. 'Right. You'd better come in then. They're talking to my mum and my sister's boyfriend. My dad'll be home from work soon.' Blah, blah, blah . . . my voice rattles on.

You see, I've suddenly remembered Ellie's words. 'Sam's *in luurve*!' All this time I'd been kidding myself that The Boy On The Train liked me too. But he didn't, of course he didn't. How could he?

He was in love with somebody else.

How could I have got it so wrong?

He's looking at you. Calm down, Flick, it's OK. Think about it. He doesn't know how you feel. As far as The Boy On The Train is concerned, you haven't given him a second thought since the minute you were whisked away by your mum.

Which is just as well. Because that boy's gone for good.

'Here's my sister coming,' I say in relief, spotting Ezzie making her way down the street towards us. I'm so fed up, the way things have turned out, I nearly add sourly, 'Looking like a Teletubby,' but I stop myself just in time. Anyway, he can see it for himself.

That's what love is like in real life. Get used to it.

Inside the house Mum and Jay are deep in conversation and Ellie is perched on the arm of the sofa inspecting Spud's dreadlocks at close quarters.

'So you two have already met!' smiles Jay.

I exchange a wry look with Sam. 'You could say that!'

'You must be Sam!' shrieks Mum and enfolds him to her, planting a smacker on his cheek. He takes it in good grace, I must say.

'Don't pretend to be nice, Mum,' I say cuttingly. 'He's already seen you at your worst.'

Mum studies him at arm's length, a tiny frown between her eyebrows. 'Have I met you somewhere before?'

'On the train to London?' I suggest sweetly. 'When you went mental?'

Mum claps her hand to her mouth. 'Oh dear. Don't tell me that was you? Honestly, Sam, I'm not normally that stressed.' She turns to Jay to explain. 'I couldn't find Flick and I went the length of that train searching for her. I thought she was going to miss the audition. We nearly did!' She turns back to Sam and beams at him. 'And you were the boy she was chatting to? Well, I never!'

Wonders will never cease.

Ellie sits suddenly bolt upright. 'Was Flick the girl you met on the train?'

'Yes,' says Sam. Ellie's face lights up as if she's about to say something and, I could be imagining it, but it seems to me an expression of alarm suddenly flickers across Sam's face. But the next second Ezzie comes in and there are introductions all round and then Mum has to interrogate her on how her exam went. Five minutes later, a bewildered Dad comes home from work to find his house flooded by his, till now, unknown extended family. Being Dad, of course, he rises admirably to the occasion and spots an opportunity for some liquid celebration. Before you can say 'long-lost cousins' he's snapping open cans right, left and centre. Jay and Sam

233

look pleasantly surprised as he thrusts beer into their hands; Spud, on the other hand, looks merely resigned.

And then, there's a knock at the door and when Mum goes to answer it, we can hear her squealing with excitement.

'I think Libby's arrived!' I say drily, still more than a bit out of sorts, if I'm honest, since I discovered I'd fallen in love with my own cousin. Mum comes back into the lounge leading Libby by the hand like a prize trophy and, behind them, looking a bit wary, are Grandma and Grandpa. It's OK though, Dad's in party-mode by now and he forgets that, actually, he's fallen out with them, and plants a kiss on Grandma's cheek, thrusts a can into Grandpa's hand, then turns his attention to Libby.

'Hi, Sis,' he says and leans forward to kiss her. 'Long time, no see.'

She smiles up at him, her eyes soft. 'You've grown a bit since I saw you last.'

Mum pats his, to be fair, practically non-existent beer belly. 'We're not too sure who's having the baby round here, him or Ezzie!'

Ezzie rolls her eyes but Dad and Libby laugh at Mum's weak joke. I know what Mum's doing, she's trying to break the ice between them. Dad's never been that enamoured with his absent older sister. As far as he's concerned, she hasn't wanted any more to do with the family since she made good. They look alike when they laugh, you can tell that they're brother and sister.

Half-brother and half-sister, I should say. I forgot Grandpa's not his father.

That makes me feel sad.

I watch as Grandpa sits down on the sofa and pats the seat next to him. Obediently, Ellie gets up and sits beside him and he puts his arm lightly round her shoulders. She snuggles comfortably into the crook of his arm and he smiles down at her.

I'm jealous. He's my granddad, not hers.

No actually. He's her granddad, not mine.

I glance around the room. Libby has moved on to talk to Ezzie now. Spud is discussing the merits of some weird band I've barely heard of with Sam. Grandma has followed Mum into the kitchen to make sandwiches and Dad is replenishing everyone's drinks.

Happy families.

Nobody needs me.

I slip out of the room and upstairs to my bedroom. On my bed, open where I left it, lies my blue notebook. Gran gave me this book to make a record of the competition.

I wish I hadn't done that flipping competition now. Then I wouldn't have gone to London in the first place and none of this would have happened.

I pick it up and start reading it. After the first page

there's hardly any mention of the competition at all. Instead, it's a record of my pathetic, non-existent, in-my-dreams love life with The Boy On The Train. From beginning to end.

I grab the pen lying next to it and score through the pages with savage, furious strokes.

I don't know how long I was up there for but it was plain to see, nobody was missing me. OK, Mum did call up to me to come and get a sandwich but I ignored her and she forgot all about me. I could hear them yacking away downstairs, making a right din, so it was obvious they were having a brilliant time without me.

Then, what seems like ages later, Ezzie sticks her head round the door. 'Come downstairs,' she says. 'Libby wants to talk to us all. I think it's important.'

'Big deal!' I mumble, my face buried in the pillow. Pretty childish, I know, but that's the way I was feeling.

'What's wrong?' says Ezzie and she sits down on the bed next to me

'Nothing!'

'Are you sulking?'

'No!'

But she can tell I'm lying. 'What's up, little Flickchick?'

she asks softly and strokes my hair. 'Feeling left out?'

I can feel the tears pricking. The next second I'm sat up and flinging my arms around her. She holds me tight and pats me comfortingly on the back, and I let the tears fall. Then I feel a sharp kick in my stomach which is squashed up against Ezzie's belly. It's as if little Chips is saying, 'Get lost, this is my mum, not yours!' and I giggle, in spite of myself. Ezzie draws back in surprise.

'He kicked me,' I explain.

'Little brute.' She eyes me carefully. 'Feeling better?'

'A bit.'

'What's the matter?'

Might as well tell her. 'It's Sam.'

'Sam downstairs?'

'He's The Boy On The Train.'

'Cousin Sam?'

I nod glumly.

'Ah!' Ezzie stares at me, wide-eyed with comprehension. 'That sucks.'

The tears threatening again.

'How does he feel about it?'

'Dunno. He probably never liked me anyway.'

'Huh!' she says. 'You reckon? That's why he keeps asking where you've got to every five minutes.'

'Does he?' I say eagerly, then sigh. 'What's the point, Ez? He's my cousin. It's not going anywhere.'

Ezzie's face screws up in concentration. 'Weren't Queen Victoria and Prince Albert first cousins? Cousins are allowed to marry each other, aren't they?'

'I don't want to *marry* him!'

'I know that, idiot. But you want to go out with him. I've got an idea! Come with me.' She gets off the bed and pads into her own room where she logs on to her computer and googles the question, *Can you marry your first cousin?* She clicks on to various sites and scrolls her way through them, until she finds one with a big long list of who you're *not* allowed to marry. We scour our way through it, making yuck noises.

'Like, who would *want* to marry their uncle?' I gasp.

'Their aunty?' says Ezzie and we collapse in a fit of giggles.

At last Ezzie turns to me triumphantly. 'There you go!' she says. 'First cousins aren't on it. It *is* legal.'

My heart lifts. 'Are you sure?'

'Yep.' She studies the information carefully. 'Though, genetically, it's not a brilliant thing to do. Were you planning to start a family?'

'Puh-lease!'

'Me neither!' she says ruefully. 'These things do happen though! No you're fine, Flicketychick. You definitely won't be breaking the law if you go out with lover boy Sam.'

'There you are!' Ellie appears at the bedroom door. 'My mum says, can you come downstairs? She's got something she wants to talk to you about.' She glances round Ezzie's room. 'Lucky thing. You've got your own computer. Mum won't let me have one.'

'Not fair, is it? I haven't got my own either. But I've got a nicer room than Ez.'

'Can I see it?'

'If you like.' I lead her into my bedroom and her face lights up in delight as she spots my crammed bookshelves.

'I *love* her!' she squeals, diving to her hands and knees and grabbing a book obviously by her favourite author. 'I've been *dying* to read this one!' She stretches out comfortably on the floor.

'Aren't you coming down to hear what your mum's got to say?' I ask, but Ellie's already in another world, head propped up on her hands. 'Leave her to it then,' says my sister and we close the door.

Downstairs, everyone's moved into the kitchen. Mum, Grandma and Libby are sitting at the table while the men are standing up, leaning against the worktops, still nursing their cans of beer. It looks like a party but feels different. Tense.

'Where's Ellie?' asks Libby.

'Reading in my room. Do you want me to fetch her?'

She shakes her head. 'No. I can explain it to her later. She's a bit young to take it in anyway.'

'Take what in?' I ask.

Grandma coughs nervously. 'We don't need to do this, Libby.'

'Do what?' Nobody's listening to me.

'Yes we do,' says Libby, her face serious. 'We should have done it years ago.'

'Well, in that case,' sighs Grandpa, 'we'd better get some more chairs. I think we may all need to sit down.'

Ezzie sinks on to the one comfy chair and Sam and I go out into the conservatory to collect some fold-up ones for the rest of us.

'What's going on?' I whisper. He shakes his head.

'I'm not sure. I think Mum's about to make some sort of grand announcement. She told your grandma it was time to set the record straight.'

'She's your grandma too!' I point out.

'Yeah, I guess she is.' He doesn't sound too chuffed about it. 'Weird.'

I glance through the window and see Grandma sitting bolt upright at the kitchen table, her back rigid. Poor thing. Who does his mum think she is, coming down here, directing us about, revealing all the family secrets? It's none of her business.

'She's a lovely gran,' I say fiercely.

Sam looks at me in surprise. 'I know. I didn't mean . . .'

'Come on, you two,' says Spud, appearing at the door. 'Everyone's waiting.'

'What's it got to do with you anyway?' I ignore Spud's startled face, grab a chair and march straight into the kitchen, placing it squarely between Grandma's and Mum's.

'Right then.' I tuck my arm through Grandma's and glare at Libby. 'We're all here. Come on then, Famous Television Controller, spill the beans.'

'Flick!' gasps Mum. 'Don't be so rude!' But Libby glances at me sympathetically before she turns to Grandma.

'This is why we need to clear things up, Mum,' she says gently. 'Everyone's barking up the wrong tree.'

Spud hands a chair to Dad and gives me a sideways look. 'Maybe I should leave,' he mumbles.

Dad frowns at him. 'What for?'

Grandma leans back and catches Spud's hand. 'Sit down, son, you're part of this family now.' Spud looks at me quickly as if he's still seeking my permission and I feel like a worm. I nod and he sits down obediently next to Ezzie.

Grandma turns to Dad. 'Martin. I'm sorry you found out you were adopted the way you did. We were wrong. We should have told you years ago.'

'Why didn't you?'

'We didn't think you'd ever need to know,' says Grandpa. 'And, anyway, we always thought of you as ours.'

I feel a lump in my throat. He's not though, is he? Not yours, Gramps, anyway. Dad must have been thinking the same thing because he gazes at his hands for a long time before he finally asks, 'Who is my father?'

Grandma and Grandpa look at each other. Nobody speaks. Then Libby clears her throat. 'I think the important point is, who is your mother?'

'I know that,' he says, his head jerking up in surprise. He indicates Grandma. 'It's Mum. It's on my birth certificate. Elizabeth Pottery.'

Grandma sighs. 'There's more than one Elizabeth Pottery, Martin.'

'There's me!' pipes up Ezzie. 'I'm Elizabeth Pottery too.'

'What?' I say, confused. '*You're* not his mother!' Nobody laughs. Slowly, my all-American uncle, Jay Ryder, unfolds his long length from the cupboard he's been leaning against and moves across to stand behind his wife. He places his hands on her shoulders.

'Where I come from,' he announces, 'Libby is a shortened form of Elizabeth.'

Next to me I feel my mother stiffen. 'It is here too,' she says, under her breath.

All eyes turn to Libby. She doesn't look in control any more. She looks small and scared. Her hand moves up to clasp her husband's.

'It's me, Martin,' she whispers. 'I'm the Elizabeth Pottery on your birth certificate. I'm your birth mother.'

'Just a boy,' she'd said. 'A schoolboy. Too young to face up to his responsibilities.'

Dad's father. The person we inherited our crazy hair from.

Grandma and Grandpa are not his parents. They're his grandparents. Which makes them my great-grandparents.

*Would you rather your grandparents turn out to be your great-grandparents or not be related to you at all?*

Your great-grandparents, of course.

Did Sam know about this? I sneak a look at him. He looks as stunned as the rest of us. Except for Jay, who must have known the whole story all along.

'You weren't much more than kids yourself,' Grandma says pensively. 'With your whole lives ahead of you.'

'She had a brilliant future predicted,' says Grandpa.

'A place at university. We didn't want her to miss out on all that.'

'So you gave me away? Just like that?' asks Dad bitterly. He addresses his words to Libby but he's refusing to look at her so he doesn't see the flash of pain in her eyes.

'It wasn't like that!' she says, but Grandma interrupts, leaping to her defence.

'It was me,' she says. 'I wanted her to go to university. I didn't get the chance so I wanted it for our Libby.'

Dad darts her a look of contempt but Grandpa says, 'If you're looking to apportion blame, Martin, don't. It was nobody's fault. We all acted in your best interests.'

'*My* best interests! She gave me up for a university place!' Dad says with scorn.

Libby winces. 'I didn't want to go!' she says wildly. 'I didn't want to leave you.'

'We persuaded her.' Grandpa's voice is sad, but matter-of-fact. 'If you lost your university place in those days you'd never get another one, not with a baby to look after. It was different then.'

'We told her to get a degree, get herself qualified, then she could support you properly. We'd look after you till then,' says Grandma. 'We couldn't let you go to strangers.'

'I never meant to give you up!' says Libby.

'So why didn't you come back for me then?' For the

first time Dad looks straight at her. Her face flushes but she meets his eyes.

'I did! I hated being away from you. I was so miserable. I couldn't wait for the end of each term to see you again, to hold you in my arms.' There is no doubting the anguish in her voice. 'Each holiday you were bigger and bonnier. You grew so fast.'

Dad stares at her, his face impatient. 'Got fed up, did you, once the novelty had worn off. Wanted to spend more time with your posh friends?'

'Of course not!' Libby's face puckers with distress. 'Believe me! It was nothing like that!'

Mum leans forward and clutches Dad's hand. 'Listen to what she's got to say, Martin.'

Libby gulps. 'As the years went by, I could see you growing closer and closer to Mum and Dad and further and further away from me. They were the only parents you knew, Martin. You loved them. And they loved you.'

'We still do,' whispers Grandma and I can feel myself welling up.

'When I finally got my degree I was offered a job in television,' continues Libby. 'I took you to London, found a woman to look after you during the day while I went out to earn a living.'

'Martin?' Mum peers up at him. 'You told us about this.'

'You were so miserable, you wouldn't eat, wouldn't sleep. When I came home from work, it wasn't me you wanted. You cried day and night for Mum and Dad till you made yourself ill.'

'I remember that,' says Dad quietly.

'What could I do?' Libby's voice breaks. 'In the end I gave in and brought you home again.'

'We decided to do it properly, for your sake. We adopted you legally, thought it was the best way,' says Grandpa.

'You see, I thought I could handle it but I was wrong,' says Libby. 'Every time I came home to see you it made it worse, I just wanted you back again.'

'It wasn't fair on you, Martin,' says Grandpa. 'You needed to know where you belonged.'

Dad nods.

'It wasn't fair on Mum and Dad either,' says Libby fiercely. 'So a job came up on American TV and I went for it. It was better to get right out of the way: to let them get on with the decent job they were doing of bringing you up, and for me to try to forget you and start again.'

'And did you? Forget him?' whispers Ezzie.

'Never.'

The whole room is silent except for a little choking sound from Ezzie and an acute nose-blowing session from Mum. Then Grandpa adds, 'We always meant to tell you the truth, son, but as the years went by, it became harder and harder. We decided in the end to let sleeping dogs lie.'

I look at Sam. He's staring at Dad. This is a hell of a thing to take in. He's suddenly discovered he's got a long-lost brother who's at least twenty years older than him.

Weird.

My heart thuds into the pit of my stomach.

Oh my goodness!

*Sam* is my father's brother.

*Sam* is my *uncle.*

*Would you rather the boy you're in love with be your cousin or your uncle?*

Neither!

Not an answer!

OK then. Cousin.

Because uncles are DEFINITELY illegal!

So, that's it, there are no more skeletons in our family cupboard. But it does mean seriously bad news for me. Bad Boy Sam and I are definitely a no-go area. It is *not* a good idea to date your dad's brother!

Not that he's even asked me.

After a while, Jay takes my grandparents home in the car, saying he'll be back later for the others. Sam sees them off at the front door. Mum, Dad and Libby take themselves into the lounge to have a private mulling over of all these disclosures. Knowing Dad, he'll need a stiff whisky from the cocktail cabinet to help it sink in. I just have time to whisper an urgent, 'It's worse than we thought. He's my *uncle*!' to Ezzie and for her to give me a sympathetic hug before Sam comes back into the kitchen. I feel a bit awkward then, I don't know what to say, but fortunately, Ezzie takes charge.

'Did you know all about this, Sam?' she asks.

'Vaguely. I sort of knew Mum had had a son adopted years ago when she was a teenager, though she never talked about it. I didn't know it was your dad though!' He raises his eyebrows. 'Weird!'

'I think it's really sad,' sighs Ezzie and her chin wobbles again. 'Your poor mum. She missed him so much, you could tell.' She gives Sam a woebegone little smile. 'She must have been so glad when you were born.'

'Um . . . No, she wasn't, actually,' says Sam.

Ezzie looks horrified. 'She was, I'm sure she was! It must have been so hard for her to give Dad up.' She looks fiercely at Spud. 'I will NEVER give up our baby!'

'I know,' he says calmly, putting his arm round her and drawing her to him. 'I knew that all along.'

Happiness burns inside me. My sister's going to keep

her baby. Nothing else matters. Not me, not Sam, not anyone. It makes me giddy, reckless. I'm curious about something and I don't care, I'm going to find out. 'Are you a bad boy, Sam?' I ask, mock-seriously.

'No!' he says, startled.

'Do you give your mum a hard time?'

'No, I don't think so. Why do you ask?'

'Something she said, when I first met her . . . about seventeen being a difficult age,' I explain.

'She was probably talking about herself,' says Spud, the voice of reason. 'It can't have been easy, being pregnant at that age.'

'It isn't,' says Ezzie, feelingly.

'She looked so sad, I assumed you must be up to no good.'

'We get on fine, Mum and me,' says Sam, bewildered.

'But,' I stare at him perplexed, 'you just said your mum didn't want you . . . ?'

'I didn't!'

'Yes you did! You said she wasn't glad when you were born.'

'Oh I see.' He grins. 'I meant she couldn't have been glad when I was born because she wasn't around to see it.'

'What?'

'Libby's not actually my mum. My own mother died

when I was a baby. I came as a package with my dad. When Libby met him in the States, she got two for the price of one.'

My heart starts thumping like I'm about to have a cardiac arrest.

'So, let's get this straight. You're not actually related to Libby at all?' says Ezzie, grinning at me wickedly.

'Not technically. I think of her as my mum though. She's the only one I've ever known. Bit like your dad and grandma.'

'What about Ellie?'

'She's Mum's.'

'I'm named Elizabeth after her,' says a voice. It's Ellie. I'd forgotten she was upstairs, oblivious to everything that's been going on down here. 'And I'm named after my grandma too.'

'Everybody's called Elizabeth in this family!' I say, beside myself with happiness now I've found out Sam and I have no blood ties whatsoever. 'It's a family tradition. You'll have to name your baby after Grandma too if it's a girl, Ez.'

'Maybe,' she says. 'Or after Grandpa if it's a boy. It's his turn.'

Albert? I hope she's joking. Ellie sidles into the kitchen, holding something behind her back. 'Flick? You met Sam before, didn't you?'

'Yes.' I smile at her happily. 'I met him on a train on the way to London.'

'Well I never!' says Ezzie, trying to keep a straight face. 'You kept that quiet!'

'Was that,' Ellie turns around and consults what she's holding behind her back, 'about six weeks ago?'

'Six weeks and five days ago actually,' I say. 'What have you got there?'

'I thought so!' She beams at Sam in excitement. 'Flick's that girl, isn't she?'

'What girl?' he says cautiously.

'The one you said you were *in lurrve* with?'

Ezzie splutters with laughter.

Sam flushes painfully to the roots of his hair. 'Ellie!' he groans and hides his head in his hands.

I think I'm going to die of happiness.

Ellie pulls my blue velvet book out from behind her back.

'Don't be embarrassed, Sam,' she says. 'You should see what she's said about you!'

I'm on the train again, this time with Dad. We're off to the Champions League Final in Italy. I've never seen him so excited in my life. He keeps taking the match tickets out of his wallet and kissing them. I've got the bag containing our clothes, wash stuff and those all-important passports and I'm not letting it out of my sight this time. Jay is going to pick us up from the station and we're staying with the Ryders overnight. I think I'm looking forward to that as much as the match. I can't wait to see them all. Especially Sam. He's taking me out for a pizza. Our first date.

Then tomorrow afternoon we meet up with Tabitha, pick up our plane tickets and fly off to Rome with her. How fantastic is that?

Sam and I have been texting all the time. Amy is green with envy. She thinks it's the most romantic thing she's ever heard of.

'I can't believe you thought he was your uncle!' she giggles. 'Uncle Sam! And he's American!'

'I don't know if it'll come to anything,' I say. 'I mean, I'm not sure I'm really in love with him, Ames. How do you know? I like him though. Loads. I can't stop thinking about him.'

'Sounds like love to me,' she says wistfully. 'I'm going to have to go on a train one day and see if I can find a fella. There was a really old film once, a black and white one, about a couple who met on a train.'

'Brief Encounter,' I say. 'My gran's favourite. It's a classic.'

Grandma! What's she like? You'll never guess what she's done! She's only gone and enrolled at the college on a course. She's got a student card and everything. She can get ten per cent off in Topshop.

It's Spud's fault. She was round our house the whole time, now that everything had been sorted out, fussing around Ezzie till it did my sister's head in. Gran was convinced she was about to go into labour any minute.

'She needs something else to think about,' said Spud and he brought her home a prospectus from the college. 'There's some good stuff in here,' he said. 'Take a look.'

Grandma laughed. 'Oh my word, I'm too old for all that.'

But Ezzie said, 'No, Gran, you should've gone to uni. It's never too late.'

They looked through it together, the three of them, and before you know it, Grandma was persuaded. I thought she'd do something like flower arranging or a cookery course but no way, she's signed up for an HND in Media Studies and Grandpa's had to buy her a brand-new 42-inch High Definition TV and Home Theatre System with wireless subwoofer. Apparently it offers the best sound and picture quality for the films she has to study.

'She's a clever woman, your grandma,' says Grandpa proudly. 'She deserves the best.'

I think our Spud's the clever one. Thanks to him, Grandma's out of Ezzie's hair, she's got a great entertainment system we can make use of, plus I've got unlimited access to a student card that gives ten per cent off at my favourite shop. The boy's a genius!

I just realized what I said. *Our* Spud. When did that happen?

Oh, and he's doing a course too. A cookery course, the one I thought Grandma would do. He's going to be a chef. He reckons it'll be a doddle after working in the kitchens. He and Grandma can be college mates.

My phone rings. Sam?

Wrong. It's Mum.

'Just to let you know,' she says, her voice high with excitement, 'Ezzie's gone into labour. The baby's on its way!'

'Oh my goodness!'

'What is it?' asks Dad in alarm.

'Ezzie's having the baby. Oh no!' I wail into the phone. 'We're going to miss it! Tell her to hang on, Mum!'

Mum laughs. 'She can't do that, love. The way things are looking, it'll be here before long. Don't worry, I'll keep you posted.'

I am *so* disappointed. 'She's having it now!' I say, snapping my phone shut. 'We're going to miss it all! It'll be a week old by the time we get home.'

Dad looks as gutted as I am.

'It's not fair!' I groan. 'Why did it have to come today of all days?'

He looks thoughtful. 'What time do we fly tomorrow?' he asks.

'Two p.m.'

He takes a train timetable out of his pocket and consults it. 'Hmm. There's a train leaving from home at five thirty in the morning that would get us to the airport on time.'

'Five thirty in the morning?' I say faintly. What I really mean is, but then I won't see Sam.

The train starts slowing down as it approaches a station.

'*Would you rather,*' Dad says slowly, reading my mind, '*see Ezzie's baby tonight or Sam?*'

Baby or Sam? Baby or Sam? Baby or Sam?

'That's my game!' I protest. 'Anyway, what if it hasn't arrived by tonight?

'*Would* you *rather see the Champions League Final or Ezzie's new baby?*'

A flicker of pain passes over Dad's face. I can practically see his brain throbbing to the rhythm of the train as he considers his choice.

Baby or Footy? Baby or Footy? Baby or Footy?

The train lurches to a stop at the station. He peers through the window.

'That train over there,' he remarks conversationally, 'is going back down the line. We could catch it if we get a move on.'

I bite my lip.

'OK then,' he says decisively. 'Sam, Footy or Baby? After three. One . . . Two . . . Three?'

'BABY!'

We leap up together but he's down the aisle and wresting the door open before I can say, 'Wait for me!' I jump down from the train in hot pursuit then immediately turn around and clamber straight back on again.

Changed my mind?

No way!

I've left the flipping bag on the train again!

I grab hold of it and chase after Dad, who is legging it over the bridge, and reach the train just as the whistle blows. He holds the door wide open for me and I hurl myself inside.

'Made it!' he says triumphantly, slamming the door shut behind us. We collapse into a seat, laughing, out of breath and extremely pleased with ourselves.

But then, as its rate returns to normal, my heart goes into a sudden dive. 'Flipping heck, Dad,' I say. 'What have we done?'

'The right thing!' he declares pompously. 'Ezzie's baby is more important than a blooming football match. Even if it is the Champions League Final . . .' His voice wavers and he looks less than convinced.

'How long was Mum in labour for?' I ask.

'Days,' he says bleakly.

We both stare glumly out at the passing countryside as we retrace the miles. My head is thudding. What if the baby doesn't come tonight? What if it doesn't come for days? We must be bonkers! I've chucked away my chance of being on the telly, Dad's blown his freebie to the Champions League Final and I've screwed up my first, perhaps my *only* date with the man of my dreams.

'Maybe we should text Ezzie and tell her to get a move on,' I say in desperation.

Dad shakes his head. 'It doesn't work like that, Flick.'

I text Sam instead to tell him the news.

Then I lapse into gloom, gazing blankly through the train window at the green fields. Overhead the sun is struggling to break through the grey clouds. What's that saying, every cloud has a silver lining? Huh! I think in my case it should be, every silver lining has a cloud!

But then Sam rings me back and tells me the date can wait, it's us that's important, not a stupid pizza, and he hopes everything goes all right for Ezzie and other really nice stuff that is too private to share . . . and the sun comes out after all and turns the world to gold.

When we've finished talking I drift away into my own happy dream world of Sam and me. So when Dad's phone bleeps in the now silent carriage, it makes me jump.

'Message from Spud,' he says and opens it up. His eyes widen.

'What is it? Has she had it?' I ask hopefully.

'Nope,' he says. 'False alarm!'

'What?' After all that! I feel like I'm about to explode. 'You are kidding me!'

'I think that's what it says.' Dad squints at the screen. 'I can't read it very well.'

'Give it to me!' I snap, and grab the phone from his hand, cursing under my breath.

And then I gasp.

I look up to see Dad watching me with the biggest, proudest, cheesiest grin plastered all over his face.

Then I read the text again, just to make sure.

It says:

BABY BOY. ALL WELL.

LOVE FROM,

EZZIE, SPUD AND ALBIE XXX

## 32C, That's Me

*Chris Higgins*

Who says you can't always get what you want?
You can if you have luck on your side.
I wanted to go out with the best-looking guy in
the school – and now I am.
I wanted the lead in the school play – and I got it.
Life doesn't get better than that.

Until one day a simple phone message turns the
best day of your life into the worst . . . and things
won't ever be the same again.

## Pride and Penalties

*Chris Higgins*

*'I rushed out of school clutcing my letter. I couldn't wait to tell Dad my news.'*

I only ever wanted my dad to be proud of me. So I'm a girl who wants to play rugby. What's wrong with that?

It's hard when your brother's constantly in the spotlight . . . but now he's got a secret of his own and so has Mum.

Being in this family is like being tangled up in a web – they don't call me Spider for nothing!

## It's a 50/50 Thing

*Chris Higgins*

With Mum on the verge of a breakdown and Dad not around anymore, Kally's new life is full of secrets.

When the gorgeous Jem skates into Kally's life and sweeps her off her feet, things finally seem to be going right.

But as Jem teaches her new tricks, Kally discovers there's more than one side to him and soon her life is spinning out of control . . .

## A Perfect Ten

*Chris Higgins*

Eva wants to be the best, just like her sister, Amber. Now she's queen of the gymnastics club, the girl everyone envies. Her life seems perfect.

But her hard work comes at a price. When new girl Patty joins the club, Eva's plans start to unravel and secrets that have long been hidden threaten to surface . . .

**Love Ya Babe**

*Chris Higgins*

Life is difficult enough for Gabby. Her parents are ancient and embarrassing, her brothers are odd and annoying and she's the only posh girl in the school.

But when her mum makes a shocking announcement and a boy comes between her and her best friend, Gabby's life becomes impossible, and soon everything starts to spin out of control . . .